THE GHOST LAKE CHRONICLES

BOOK II   THE ZORRO CLUB

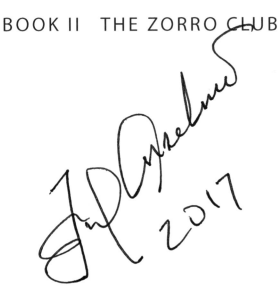

Frank D. Anselmo

Once again, I dedicate this book to my wife Noreen, my seven children, sixteen grandchildren, my many close friends, and the many people who have read book I and encouraged me to publish this book. I hope you enjoy reading this as much as I have enjoyed writing it.

Special thanks to Branden Apitz of Aluna Design for his fantastic work on the cover design.

TABLE OF CONTENTS

THE GHOST LAKE CHRONICLES

BOOK II- THE ZORRO CLUB

BLACK BAT LEADER

❊ ❊ ❊

The sun had only been set for an hour when the September harvest moon rose over the quiet little town of Ghost Lake, Minnesota. Slowly the big orange globe climbed over the trees and shined its pale light down on the lake and the houses and streets bordering it.

High up on Taylor's hill an owl hooted and opened his wings to catch the breeze blowing in from Ghost Lake. Slowly he glided down the hill toward the edge of town and landed in a tall pine tree in the Ghost Lake Cemetery. Turning his head in a full circle he could see the dark woods that marched right up to the edge of town and turning the other way he could see almost all the way up first avenue to Main street.

This is the way it was in 1952. A quiet little town with all the modern conveniences, yet the wild animals of the forest were only a stone's throw away and occasionally wandered into the very town itself.

Here and there, a short way from town, were scattered a few small farms. Usually they consisted of a house, a barn, a shed, and an occasional orchard of apples. Maybe there would be a cow, a pig or two and a few chickens, but none of them were what you could call big farms.

The town itself was not very big with a population of 1,862 men, women, and children. Going down Main Street on one side, one would walk by the Rialto movie theater, Miller's Hardware, Mary's Cafe, and Reed's Drug store. Across the street on the corner was Morgan's Chevrolet, the only car dealer in town. In the showroom window facing the street was a brand new Bel Air Chevrolet advertised for $1,800. Next to their used car lot was the Red and White Grocery, Benson's Clothing, and the Ghost Lake Liquor store. Farther down on the next block were scattered the local dentist office, Fred Bircher's Insurance Agency, Gino's Barber Shop, the newspaper office, and the village hall which housed the police station.

At this point Main Street climbed up the slope of the hill to finally come to rest in front of the Ghost Lake Public Schools. On the right was Marshall High School and on the left, separated by the playground, was E.J. Tibbets Elementary School.

Silent swings hung on big shiny steel poles in the darkened playground, resting before the rush of children and another school day. The bright moonlight reflected off the freshly painted seats and winked up at the surrounding houses as if to tell the kids that they were ready when they were. It had only been two weeks since the beginning of school and already they were showing the signs of wear, but still in much better shape than they would be by next June.

One block over on Oak Street, a light glowed from a second story window of the Bigsley house. Randy closed his notebook and glanced out the window at the moon coming up over Taylor's hill. Reflecting on the past several weeks, he smiled and tapped his pen on the notebook cover. He wondered if it was too late in the evening to call Scooter.

He sat down at his study desk and opened the top drawer. Reaching in, he pulled on a string, releasing the locking mechanism on his secret, false bottomed, second drawer. This done, he opened the second drawer and lifted out a few papers and odds and ends. He then lifted up the false panel on the bottom and placed his blue notebook in the narrow space. Closing the drawer, he once again opened the top drawer and pulled the string to lock it once more.

Going to the top of the stairs he called down. "Mom, what time is it?"

Mom's answering call came back. "It's about seven-ten...Why?"

"Could Scooter come over for awhile?"

"Oh...I guess. If it's all right with Aunt Carrie"

Randy smiled as he came down the stairs two at a time. He loved to call Scooter and talk in their pre-arranged code. Picking up the phone he hurriedly dialed and listened for the answer.

"Hello, Aunt Carrie? This is Randy. Do you think Scooter could come over for a few minutes?"

"Hi Randy, I guess he could come over for awhile, but not later than eight...Here, I'll let you talk to him."

Scooter picked up the phone and said "Hello."

On the other end, Randy lowered his voice and said, "This is Black Bat Leader to Eagle One. Do you read me?"

Scooter also lowered his voice and glanced over his shoulder to see if his mom was near. "This is Eagle One. I read you loud and clear."

"This is Black Bat Leader. The moon is over the mountain and the river is open."

Scooter knew that this meant that Randy wanted to see him and that he had already asked his mom. With a wide grin he spoke the coded answer. "The sheep are in the meadow and the cows are in the corn." Which translated meant, 'I'll be right over.'

Hanging up the phone, he turned and asked his mom. "Mom, can I go over to Randy's for a few minutes?"

Aunt Carrie, who always insisted on proper English said, "I don't know. Can you?"

Scooter wrinkled his nose and knew he had been caught again. "May I?" he corrected.

"O.K., but I want you home at eight."

"Gotcha!" Scooter said as he grabbed his jacket and headed for the door. "See you at eight."

As Scooter walked up the street he checked his jacket pocket and found his small flashlight. He snapped it on to check the battery and finding it in working order, slipped it back into his pocket. He knew that Randy, or Black Bat Leader, would be waiting for him when he turned the corner of his street.

Scooter stopped at the corner of Oak and third, looked up and down the street and saw that all was quiet. He quickly turned the corner and trotted along the sidewalk to the third elm tree. Here he stepped off and slid along behind the tree. Glancing out, he checked again to see if anyone was around. It was all clear. Digging in his pocket, he brought out his flashlight and stuck his head out from around the tree and looked at Randy's darkened window, two doors down. Pointing his flashlight up at the window, he flashed two short flashes and one long one.

Up in the dark room, Randy sat by the window, waiting for the signal from Eagle One. There it was! Two short flashes and one long! Randy grinned as he picked up his flashlight and answered with two long flashes and one short. The opposite signal meant that the coast was clear and to come ahead.

Scooter saw the answering signal and walked up to Randy's front door.

Once again he looked around before giving the secret knock. Two quick knocks followed by three with short pauses. Identical taps came from the other side of the door and Randy pulled it open.

"Hey…what's up?" Scooter said as he came in the door. "What's the deal?"

"Code Red." Randy answered, which meant that what he had to discuss was only to be said in private. "Let's go up to my room."

Once in the room, Randy took a butter knife and slipped it between the doorframe and the wall, creating a simple but effective lock. He then turned to Scooter and whispered. "The Zorro file is complete."

Scooter grinned. He knew that Randy had been working on this for a couple of weeks and was more than anxious to see it. "All right! Can I see it?" He exclaimed.

"O.K., but remember…It's for your eyes only. If this ever fell into enemy hands we'd both be goners."

"Right!" said Scooter. "I swear by the blood of Zorro that it'll only be seen by me."

Randy turned and went to his study desk. He did his thing with the string again and opened the secret compartment of the second drawer. Reaching in, he pulled out the blue notebook and handed it to Scooter.

Scooter took the notebook and read the title on the cover. **"The Zorro Club-Top Secret."**

"When did you finish?" he asked in a low voice.

"I finished today, after school." Randy replied.

"Wow! You are one fast writer! This would take me about two years and I still wouldn't have written it like you can."

This was the second notebook that Randy had filled. The first one being the one in which he had told of their summer adventure with Gramps. Scooter hoped that this story would be as good as their first one.

"Can I take it home and read it?" Scooter asked.

Randy wrinkled up his nose and thought for a moment. Finally he answered, "I suppose...but you have to guard it with your life."

"I swear, I'll chew it up and swallow it before I let it fall into enemy hands."

"Where are you going to hide it?" Randy asked.

"I'll hide it in the box spring of my bed. There's a hole in the end of it where I put stuff when I don't want it to be found."

"Does your mom know about it?"

"No, I made the hole myself and I have it hidden so you can only see it from under the bed."

"O.K., but don't leave it lying around by mistake or anything."

"Don't worry...I'm in this as much as you are. Anyway, I think things have cooled off quite a bit by now, but I'll still be careful."

Randy dug in a box he had pulled out from under his bed. Standing up, he handed Scooter a small pile of comic books. "Here, hide the notebook in between the comics and if anyone asks, you just came over and borrowed some comics from me."

"Hey, that's a neat idea!" Scooter said, sliding the notebook in about halfway down the pile. "This is just like the real spy stories!"

"Yeah," Randy said. "And you know what happens to spies when they get caught."

Scooter lowered his voice and asked. "Should I sneak out the back door and cut through the alley?"

"No, I don't think so. That would make you suspicious. Just go out the front door and walk down the street like you had come over to borrow some comics."

"Right!" Scooter said as he put the comics under his arm and went out the bedroom door. "See you in school."

At the bottom of the stairs Scooter called. "Good night Aunt Aimee...see you soon."

"Good night Scooter." She called.

TOP SECRET

❖ ❖ ❖

Scooter slipped out the front door and forced himself to walk at a normal pace down the street to his house. Twice he imagined that someone was following him and once he thought that he had seen someone hiding behind some bushes. He continually picked up the pace until by the time he had reached his house he was jogging.

Quickly he ran up to his bedroom and slid the pile of comics under the bed. He then went back downstairs, picked up the phone and dialed Randy's number. The phone hadn't finished the first ring when Randy picked it up.

"This is Black Bat Base." The voice said into the phone.

"The Eagle has landed." Scooter said and hung up the phone.

Stepping into the living room, Scooter said to his mom. "Hi mom, I'm back...I'm going to go up and do some homework before I turn in."

"All right honey, good night."

Scooter couldn't believe it...she didn't ask any questions! Here he had dreamed up this little story of how he had been over to Randy's and borrowed some comics and that now he had some homework and was a little tired and would turn in early. Oh well...it always was hard to get her attention when she was listening to her favorite radio program. It was just as well. He could hardly wait to get his hands on the blue notebook.

Safely up in his room, Scooter quickly undressed, put his pajamas on, and climbed into bed with the notebook. He reached behind his head and snapped on his bed lamp. Reaching over to the little table by his bed, he picked up a red plastic pistol that shot little darts with rubber suction cups on the end. He carefully took aim at a coke bottle sitting on the edge of his dresser. A long string tied to the top of the coke bottle, ran up the wall to an eye screw and then over at a right angle to the pull string of his ceiling light. His first shot was high and to the right. The next one was right on target and Scooter grinned as the coke bottle tumbled off the edge, pulling the string and shutting the light off before stopping two inches from the floor.

He then squirmed down under the covers and bunched his pillow up until he was comfortable. Satisfied at last, he picked up the blue notebook and once again read the cover. **THE ZORRO CLUB-TOP SECRET.** You sure had to give Randy credit; he thought to himself, he sure had a way with words.

Scooter opened the cover and read the top line of the first page. **THE GHOST LAKE CHRONICLES - BOOK II-THE ZORRO CLUB**. Beneath was the date September 21, 1952, and an author's note. The book you are about to read is true, although it may not seem possible. I, Randy Bigsley have Scooter Dobson as my true and sworn witness.

This story begins a few days before school starts in the autumn of 1952. Scooter Dobson, my cousin and best friend is new in town and is very nervous about starting school in a strange town. I guess I can't blame him as I would hate to have to go to a new town and start school all over again in a strange place. But first of all, let me give you a little background on Scooter. Scooter is his name and he is sort of tall for a kid twelve years old. He's red-headed with a crew cut and has more than a few freckles. He's usually wearing a wide grin and has a twinkle in his eyes that gives away the fact that he's always scheming and thinking of new things to do. I have to hand it to Scooter; he has this uncanny ability to come with some wild ideas about solutions to problems. The kid has an imagination!

I guess this story really began when Scooter and I were sitting up in my room a few days before school started. I was trying to reassure Scooter about starting school in a new town, but I wasn't too sure I was making much of an impression on him.

"You're not really a stranger." I explained to him. "You know me and you've met a couple of the other kids."

"I know..." Scooter said, trying to accept it. "But, you don't know what it's like. This is the third school I've moved to and it seems like it gets harder each time."

"I think you're over reacting. Most of the kids here are really nice and will want to make friends with you Sure, you'll find a few jerks, but I'll bet you will find them in any school."

"And how!" Scooter exclaimed. "I've seen them all, and it seems like the jerks always want to tangle with me."

"Well, I think you'll do just fine. Miss Williams is going to be our teacher and I've never heard anyone complain or say anything bad about her."

"It's not Miss Williams I'm worried about." Scooter continued. "I've always gotten along good with my teachers."

"See!" I pointed out. "I told you it won't be so bad. Just think. It would have been a lot worse if you had come in the middle of the year."

"Yeah, I did that once and that was something else. I guess you're right. If a guy has to move, now is a better time than most and having you as my cousin and best friend is a lot better than coming in cold turkey."

"You just wait. In a couple of weeks you'll be laughing about this and wondering what the big deal was. It's going to be a fun year. Next year we'll be going over to the junior high and things will be a lot different again."

"Yeah," said Scooter, lost deep in thought. "Our last year in elementary...I almost hate to see it end."

"You know," I admitted, "I guess you're right. It's been a lot of fun and next year people will expect different things from you, like they expect you to grow up instantly or something."

"Oh well," Scooter said, trying to change the subject. "I'll worry about that next year. Right now I want to know more about the sixth grade. How many boys are in our class?"

"Lets see..." I said, counting on my fingers, "I think with you there will be twelve or thirteen. I haven't heard of any others moving in or of any moving away."

"How many girls are there?"

"None." I said with a sober face.

"What!" Scooter yelled. "No Girls?"

I fell on the bed laughing. "Yes, there are girls. I was only kidding. Let's see...I think there's about nine or ten."

"Do you like any of them? You know, like a girlfriend." Scooter asked teasingly.

"No!" Randy exclaimed. "I'm good friends with Shelly Patten...but only friends. She lives across the alley and we've been friends since before kindergarten."

Scooter continued with his questions. "What about Arnold? Did you ever get along with him?"

I lay back on the bed and thought about that one for a few seconds. "Yeah, I think Arnold and I got along just fine for about the first hour of the first day of kindergarten and then something went wrong and we have been enemies ever since."

"Who are his friends, or should I ask, does he have any friends?"

"Oh yeah, he has friends." I assured him. "Let's see...Bird legs Lewis and Gary Grogan are probably his best friends and then there are a couple of other kids that hang around with him from time to time."

"Why do they call him bird legs?" Scooter asked.

I had to laugh at that. "Because he has these long skinny legs like a bird."

"I see. What about Arnold? Have you ever had a fight with him?" Scooter asked.

"No, but I've come awful close a few times."

"Well, what does he do to bug you?" Scooter asked.

"Anything he can." I answered. "Remember when he stole our tools when we were camping? It's stuff like that that he does. He just goes out of his ways to do mean things to kids, not just me. If he can make someone miserable, then he's happy and he really likes to put down kids for things that they can't help. Like if someone is kind of poor and doesn't have the best clothes or house or if they are kind of chubby or don't look like Arnold thinks they should, then he'll tease them and put them down."

"Wow," said Scooter. "He sounds like a real bully, but I think I'll try to give him a chance. Maybe he's changed or grown up a little."

"That's fine Scooter." I told him. "You give it your best shot. More power to you if you can be friends with him, but I wouldn't bet the farm on it."

"Well anyway," Scooter said, "It sounds like it's going to be an interesting year."

"Yeah, I get that feeling too. That's why I'm going to keep a journal. It'll be fun to go back and read in a few years. In the meantime, don't worry about the first day of school. I'm sure you'll do just fine and most of the kids will like you. I'm even a little nervous myself, but I know that everyone is and we'll all be in the same boat."

"I hope so," Scooter said. "I just wish the first week was over with and all of this was behind us."

FIRST DAY JITTERS

Scooter was still nervous as we walked up the front steps of Tibbets Elementary. He had completely forgotten everything that I had told him and had let panic overcome him instead. I had to admit, I was a little nervous myself. After all, it was the first day of school and it was only natural that a kid would be nervous. For one thing, I hadn't seen some of these kids for the whole summer and it was a little awkward thinking of what to say when you first met.

Some of the kids had arrived a little earlier than we did and were recalling the good times of the last school year. Having gotten over their summer jitters, they were warmed up and ready to deliver their wisecracks to the new arrivals. I had warned Scooter of this good natured teasing and we had more or less prepared ourselves for it.

Ronnie Franzen took the first shot. "Hey Randy!" He called. "Where you been hiding all summer...at Girl Scout Camp?"

Luckily I remained cool under fire and was able to think fast and shoot back with out losing face. "Hey Ronnie! No, I tried to sign up for the camp, but they told me you had taken the last opening."

The rest of the guys laughed hard at that one. I had done it. I had broken the ice with one blow and we settled into a normal conversation.

"Listen up guys!" I said, calling upon their attention. "I want you to meet Scooter Dobson, my cousin and a good friend."

"That's cool," Piped in Ritchie Kramer, "Most people's cousins live too far away to be friends."

It was as easy as that. Scooter walked around the group of boys shaking hands while trying to remember their names. I had described a few of them beforehand and Scooter was quick to pick up on their names.

It was just as I had predicted. The boys had taken to him right away and had accepted him as one of us. It was only natural, as Scooter was warm, friendly, and quick witted enough to come back on wisecracks. We had a good time on the front steps of Tibbets Elementary...that is, until Arnold showed up with a couple of his cronies.

He really thought he looked cool as he swaggered up the sidewalk in a black leather jacket and his shiny black hair slicked back with about a pound of grease. Stopping about five feet away, his eyes shifted around our crowd, stopping for a moment on each of us. His mouth was half open and his lower lip stuck out a little, like he was about to say something but was considering whether we were worthy of it or not.

Finally, he decided to honor us with a statement. "Hey guys...what's up?"

Johnny Tyson, ever the nice guy, tried to warm up the situation by introducing Scooter to Arnold. "Hi Arnold, Have you met Scooter, Randy's cousin?"

The rest of the guys didn't know it, but Scooter and I had already had a run in with Arnold a few weeks back during our camping trip. Arnold had come out on the short end of a bet we had made and had not spoken to us since. Now, here with his friends to back him, he decided to get in a few jabs.

"We've met." Arnold sneered, and then added. "...And if he stays out of my way, he may make it to the end of the school year."

The boys all looked uncomfortably at Scooter. What was he going to do? It was showdown time. Either Scooter made an attempt at standing up to him or was forced to take his dirt for the rest of the year. Scooter was cool.

He looked at Arnold for a few seconds with a wrinkled forehead...like he didn't recognize him. "Arnold...Arnold.." He said, trying to recall. He took a slow step to Arnold's side and peeked around the back of his head. "Oh yeah, I remember you now. You're hair is different than it was a couple of weeks ago."

Reaching out, Scooter touched his finger to the side of Arnold's head, ran it down an inch or so, and then examined it closely. Shaking his head slowly, he turned to Arnold and said. "I hate to tell you this Arnold, but I think you're due for an oil change."

He had done it! Not only had he destroyed Arnold with the greatest put down possible, but he had done it in front of most of the sixth grade boys, making it the double greatest! Every boy there, with the exception of Arnold and his friends, collapsed in gales of laughter. Tears rolled from their eyes as they thought of what Scooter had said and wished that they had had the guts to say. There was no doubt. Scooter was in like Flynn.

Arnold, having lost face and not being quick enough for a comeback, did the next best thing. He shook his head at us, like we were slime or something and shouldered his way past and up the steps to the school.

Scooter just stood there and grinned as the rest of us slowly regained control of ourselves. I guess Ritchie Kramer summed it up best as he put an arm around Scooter's shoulder and said, "You're o.k. Dobson! That was like Rocky Marciano knocking out Joe Louis with one punch!"

The school bell rang to officially announce the beginning of another school year. All of us, pretending that we dreaded coming back, trudged up the steps and into the school. The smell of fresh varnish hit me as we walked down the main hall and up the steps to the sixth grade room. Some of the kids were in the room, picking out their desk, while another bunch milled around in the hall.

I nudged Scooter. "Stick close to me...I'll introduce you to Miss Williams." Having been in this school for six years already, counting kindergarten, I sort of knew Miss Williams and had talked to her on more than one occasion.

Miss Williams was seated at her desk, surrounded by three or four girls. She was wearing a pale blue, flowered dress and her pretty blond hair was pulled back in a bun.

"Good morning boys," she said as we approached her desk.

"Good morning Miss Williams," I answered. "I'd like you to meet my cousin, Scooter. He'll be in our class this year."

"I'm pleased to meet you." She said extending her hand, "I assume that Scooter is not your real name."

"No ma'am," Scooter answered quite nervously. "My real name is Leonard, but hardly anyone calls me that. Even my mom calls me Scooter and I would sure appreciate it if you could also."

"I see..." Miss Williams said slowly. "Hmmm...Well, we'll have to see."

Scooter took this opportunity to butter Miss Williams up a little. He is such a con artist! "I hope so...," he began. "I'm sure this is going to be a great year. I've heard a lot of good things about you Miss Williams, but nobody told me that you were so young and pretty."

Miss Williams blushed and stammered, "Well...ah...thank you...um...Scooter. That's very nice of you to say."

"You're welcome ma'am."

I smiled to myself. Scooter was such a con artist!

All of the kids had come into the room now and Miss Williams stood up and tinkled a little bell that she had on her desk. "Children..." She called, waiting for the room to quiet down. "Welcome back for another school year. I would like all of you to find a desk that fits you for now. Later I will arrange the seating according to what works best."

Everyone bustled around the room trying to find a desk that fit them best, while at the same time being close to one of their best friends. Within a few minutes every desk was filled and as luck would have it, Scooter was across the aisle and one seat back from me. I knew from experience that this was probably too good to last, but for the time being it was good enough.

We spent the rest of the morning passing out books and having our book numbers recorded in Miss Williams' record book. We also paged through each book and discussed what we were going to be studying in the coming year. Before I knew it, the morning had passed and the noon hour bell was ringing.

"What do you think Scoot?" I asked as we walked down the two flights of stairs to the cafeteria in the basement.

"I think it's going to be o.k." Scooter answered. "Miss Williams is nice, the kids are nice and if the food is good it'll be all that I can ask for."

"You're in for a surprise." I assured him as we lined up in the hall outside the cafeteria. "Mrs. Sordi is the best cook in three states. I hope she cooked Spanish rice today. That's my favorite."

Mrs. Sordi hadn't cooked Spanish rice, but we did have mashed potatoes with hamburger gravy, homemade bread, peach sauce for dessert and all the milk we could drink. Twenty minutes later we finally brought up our dirty dishes and walked out to the playground.

"Man!" Scooter commented as we stood outside the building. "If Mrs. Sordi cooks like that every day, they'll be calling me Chubby by the end of the school year."

Arnold happened to be coming out the door right behind us and heard Scooter's comment. True to form, he couldn't say anything nice. "You call that slop food? I wouldn't feed that to my dog!"

Arnold brushed by us before we could say a word. Scooter just shook his head and asked. "What is with that kid? Is he ornery like this all the time?"

"No Scooter," I assured him. "Sometimes he's worse."

We spent the remainder of the noon hour visiting with some of the other guys and throwing a softball around. Soon the afternoon bell rang and once more we were back in the classroom.

The first forty five minutes of the afternoon were spent reviewing our spelling workbooks and studying the list of words for the week. Miss Williams told us to write each word five times and do the first page of the workbook. She then told us that the first spelling test of the year would be on Friday and that we would be having a spelling test on each Friday until the end of the year. Miss Williams then announced that she had a special assignment for the first day of the school year. "I'd like all of you children to take out a paper and pencil and do a little writing." She said.

"I would like you to organize an outline of an event that you took part in during the summer. This could be a trip with your parents, a day at the beach, a visit from some relatives, or just a fun time that you had with some of your friends. In a half hour we will take this outline and use it to tell the class about your particular story."

This was too good to be true! I knew that our camping trip story would be far and above any story anyone could tell. All I had to do was to convince Miss Williams to let me and Scooter do it together. I thought about it for a minute before I approached Miss Williams at her desk.

"Umm...Excuse me Miss Williams, but Scooter and I have a problem. You see, we both have the same story to tell and I was wondering...if you would let us work on this together."

"Well, I don't usually let children do this; but, since it's the first day and Scooter is new here, I guess I'll let you work together."

"Thank you ma'am." I said as I turned and walked back to my seat with a big smile. I quickly huddled with Scooter for a minute or so as we quickly reviewed our story and decided to divide it into two parts. I would tell the first part and Scooter the second. We had decided to just keep the story to the camping part and not reveal the legend of Ghost Lake or the secret we had discovered.

MARK OF THE Z

❖ ❖ ❖

The next half hour flew by as I quickly sketched an outline of my part of the story. I tried to make it as exciting and as humorous as possible and yet let it lead naturally into Scooter's second part. I put the finishing touches on it just as Miss Williams announced that we would now have the story time.

She began by asking for volunteers and naturally, nobody wanted to be first. Miss Williams finally gave up and called on Mary Woods, whom Miss Williams had known from last years Christmas program which she directed. Mary was not bashful and had what Gramps called the gift of gab. She marched right up and told of her two week stay with her cousin in Minneapolis. It was not very exciting.

After Mary, everyone seemed to have confidence and hands were being raised all over the room. I felt that our story, being one of the best, should be saved for one of the last, so I kept my hand down and let the rest of the class tell their tales.

Art Hill told a pretty good one about how he and his Uncle had gone fishing at Leech Lake. His Uncle hooked a huge Muskie and they fought it for two hours before landing it. It weighed in at thirty-two pounds, or so Art said. Knowing Art, I would guess that he probably added five or ten pounds, but it was a good story.

Johnny Tyson told about a big wreck he saw on the highway, where a cattle truck tipped over in the ditch and killed six cows. Kathy Johnson told of how a big bear had broken into her Uncle's chicken house and had killed off a bunch of the chickens. All in all, the stories were pretty good and the afternoon was flying by.

Finally it was down to me, Scooter, and Arnold. I felt that now was the time as the rest of the class was warmed up and ready for a great conclusion.

I began with how I had been in the woods building my tree fort. From there I told of how Scooter, hearing me pounding nails, had come into the woods and visited me at my fort. I explained of how well we hit it off and then how we had come up with the idea of camping out. I told of clearing the campsite, planning and preparing, and setting up camp. At this point I stopped and introduced Scooter to tell the second half of our adventure.

Scooter was a natural story teller. He began with a description of how night fell on our little campsite and of the noises we heard in the woods. The class hung on each word as Scooter began telling of the thunderstorm and of how Blanca, Scooter's dog, crawled into the tent with us. When everyone was on the edge of their seat, he brought the story to a climax by telling of how when Blanca was growling at something outside of the tent, we had tied two firecrackers together and thrown them out the tent door. The final blow came when Scooter explained of how Blanca, being afraid of firecrackers had jumped backward, knocking the tent down around us.

The class howled with laughter while Scooter walked back to his seat.It was a great beginning for Scooter! Everyone seemed to like him and I knew in my heart that he would have no trouble getting along at Tibbets Elementary.

The only one left was Arnold and I was more than curious as to what he was going to tell. He just sat there and let the class settle down before he stood up and walked to the front of the class.

"All right class!" Miss Williams called. "Let's settle down and let Arnold tell his story." Glancing up at the clock, she added. "There's only a half hour left in the day. So, when Arnold is finished, we'll go out on the playground for the remainder of the afternoon."

Arnold was once again Mr. Cool. He looked over the class for a few seconds before beginning. "What I have to tell...is not going to take very long...because most of it is secret.

With this statement Arnold had everyone's attention. Most of the boys looked at each other with raised eyebrows, waiting for Arnold to continue.

Arnold paused and looked the class over slowly, then continued. "A few of us boys have started a club and we are not letting anyone else in. The only thing I can tell you is that we have a club house in a secret place and we do things that can't be told to anyone outside of the club. I'm sure you will be hearing about us and talking about us during the year, but you'll never know for sure if it is us that you're hearing about." At this point Arnold paused to let it sink in, and then continued.

"I can only tell you two things about our club. One...is that I'm the president, and the other is...that our name is... The Black Skulls."

With that, Arnold turned on his heel and walked slowly back to his seat. I had to admit it, Arnold had landed a blow with this short story that none of us could top. He had the whole class wondering what the club was, where it met, who was in it, and what they did.

Arnold the rat had done it! He had managed to steal all of the thunder from our camping story. You could just feel the jealousy hanging in the air of the classroom. Scooter and I had managed to go from glory to gloom in three short minutes. Not one kid was thinking of what we had said or done. They were wondering and wishing they knew what Arnold's club was and what they did.

Luckily Miss Williams broke the mood by announcing, "All right class, those were all very interesting stories. Now, as I promised, we'll go out on the playground for the last half hour."

"What a creep that Arnold is!" I said as we walked out the door. "Why didn't we think of that, Scooter?"

"Big deal!" Scooter snarled. "I wouldn't join that jerks club if he asked me!"

"Jerk?" I asked. "I thought you were going to try to be friends with him."

"Are you kidding? After today, there's no way I'd be his friend."

"But you said you'd give him a chance." I teased.

"He had his chance." Scooter said stubbornly.

"Well..." I continued, "I still wish we had thought of it first. It sounds like it'd be a lot of fun."

"So?" Scooter argued. "Is there some law against starting our own club?"

"Hey! That's right!" I suddenly realized. "That's a super idea! Let's get together after school tonight and make some plans."

"Sounds good to me." Scooter said with a grin, "In the meantime, let's be thinking of some names for the club and who we'll have in it."

"All right! We'll show Arnold what a real club is!"

After school, I sat up in my room and thought about our club. I don't know why, but my mind was a blank. I guess I was thinking too much about Arnold and his club. I was hoping that Scooter had come up with an idea. He always seemed to have some ideas and I was sure that he wouldn't fail me now.

Shortly after supper, Scooter showed up and we went up to my room to work out the details of our club. "Well Scooter," I asked, "What did you come up with?"

"I was just going to ask you the same question." Scooter said. "I haven't been able to think of anything."

"Oh great! I thought you'd have it all figured out by now."

"Don't panic. I'm sure we'll think of something." Scooter assured me.

I glanced at the clock on my dresser. "Hey, it's almost time for Zorro. Let's listen to it and think about the club later. Our brains need a rest anyway."

"O.K." Scooter said, "Tonight's the night we find out who's been robbing those people in that little town."

"I'll bet Zorro's got that figured out already, but the people will never know he's involved."

"Yeah," said Scooter. "That's the neat thing about Zorro. He always helps the good guys and they never know who he is."

"But..." I added, "They know it was Zorro who helped them because of the mark of the Z, but they don't know who Zorro is. Let's go."

A few minutes later found us in front of the big radio in the living room, tuned in to the continuing story of Zorro. There were rumors around town that in a couple of years we would be able to watch these radio programs on television. I had read about television in a Popular Mechanics magazine, but couldn't imagine having one in our house. Besides, someone said that they would cost over four hundred dollars and that was about what my dad made in two months work, and anyway I thought, it couldn't be any more exciting than listening to a program on the radio.

Tonight's program was, as usual, a combination of mystery, suspense, and drama, with Zorro coming out the hero once again. He managed to put away the bad guys and leave unnoticed, except for the mark of the Z. Like the Lone Ranger, he left the townspeople wondering who that hero was.

As the music faded I walked over and shut the radio off. Turning back, I saw Scooter sitting on the couch with a wide grin and a faraway look in his eyes. "What're you grinning about?" I asked, knowing that he probably had something up his sleeve.

"Let's go back to your room." Scooter suggested.

Once back in my room, Scooter carefully closed the door and whispered. "That's it! Don't you see?"

I frowned at Scooter. "No...I don't see. What're you talking about?"

"Our club!" Scooter said impatiently. "We can be like Zorro and do good deeds without anyone knowing who did it."

I thought about it for a few seconds and it sounded like a good idea. "Great Idea Scoot! And we could even call ourselves the Zorro's and leave the mark of the Z with paint or something."

"Right! Let's see...we have a name and we have a purpose. Now we have to have a secret meeting place and meeting times."

"How about my old tree house in my back yard by the alley? We could meet up in there and nobody would know about it. Shall we get some more guys to join?"

"I don't know..." Scooter pondered. "I'm afraid if we get more guys, it'll be too hard to keep it secret."

"That's true," I agreed. "Anyway, we'll start out with just you and me and if we want to later, we can ask someone else to join."

"What'll we do for good deeds?" Scooter asked.

"I'm not sure...Let's go out and ride around town on our bikes and look for some ideas. If you spot something that will work, raise your right hand and make the mark of the Z."

"Neat idea!" Scooter agreed. "Then, after we decide on a target, we'll get together and make up a plan."

"Yeah, let's go! There's still about an hour of daylight left."

MISSION ONE

❖ ❖ ❖

We jumped on our bikes and began to slowly cruise down the street toward the school. We weren't sure what we were looking for, but were hoping that an idea would turn up. After two blocks, Scooter pulled his bike over to the side of the street and turned to me.

"Let's ride through a few alleys and see if we can turn up something."

"O.K." I said, "But let's split up and ride separately. We'll be able to cover more territory that way. I'll ride the alley on this block and you ride the alley one block down from me. When we get to the street side on the other end we'll wait for the other to come out. If either of us spots a target, we'll wave the sign of the Z to each other."

"Sounds good! Let's go."

I didn't find anything worthwhile in the first alley and apparently Scooter didn't either, as I didn't get any signal from him.

Scooter was the first one out of the next alley and it was apparent that he had found something as he was frantically waving the sign of the Z as I came out the end of my alley.

Not even stopping, I turned my bike and pedaled as fast as I could down to where he was waiting with a big grin on his face.

"What'd you find?" I quickly asked.

"Follow me." Scooter said with a jerk of his head.

Slowly we cruised up the alley until we came to a red faded fence. Scooter looked over his shoulder at me, pointed at the yard and made the sign of the Z, and kept on riding.

I stopped pedaling and coasted by the yard Scooter had pointed at. An old man was in the back yard working. He was taking firewood from a large pile and stacking it in a neat row along his side fence. I wasn't sure, but I thought it was Johnny Tyson's grandfather.

Scooter was waiting for me at the other end of the alley. I pulled up alongside of him and waited for him to speak.

"Did you see the old man piling firewood?" He asked.

"Yeah, what's the plan?"

"Well, the way I figure it, we'll have to work fast on this one. If we wait until tomorrow night, he'll be done with the woodpile. It's going to be dark in an hour and we can come back here and finish his job for him."

That wasn't quite how I had figured the Zorro's would work. I was expecting some big elaborate planning session with maps and code words and secret messages. But, Scooter was right. If we waited to do all the planning, the job would be done by the time we got to it.

"Sounds simple enough," I agreed, "But how are we going to manage to get out of our houses long enough to do this without telling our parents?"

"Well, we can tell our parents that we are over at each others house studying for a test and then we'll come over here and do it. It shouldn't take more than an hour with both of us working."

"I suppose it would work, but I don't like the idea of lying to our parents. If either of them happened to call the others house we'd be caught and then the fur would fly."

"I know what you mean," Scooter agreed. "I don't like lying either, but remember, this is for a good cause, and besides, it wouldn't be any fun if there wasn't some risk involved."

"I suppose you're right..." I admitted. "Let's go. It'll be dark by the time we come back."

In a half-hour we had managed to go to both of our house and stumble through our story of how we had to study for this big test. Just as we stepped off of Scooter's back porch, the street lights came on; signaling that it was time for the Zorro's to do their thing.

Even without the elaborate plans it was an exciting moment. We had decided to leave our bikes at home and sneak in on foot as this called for the greatest of secrecy. At the last moment Scooter had thought about our wearing dark clothing and had even managed to find two black stocking caps for us to wear.

By the time we arrived at the entrance to Grandpa Tyson's alley it was almost totally dark, as the moon hadn't risen yet.

Scooter glanced up at the black sky and whispered, "Perfect!"

We took one last look up and down the street before slipping into the alley. You never know when you might be be followed by some intruder or spy. I nodded to Scooter that it was all clear from my end and the mission began.

We stayed close to the edge of the alley and slowly made our way down to Grandpa Tyson's fence. Here we got down on our hands and knees and crawled for a few yards to a place where there was a wide crack in the fence. We slowly raised our heads over the fence and surveyed the yard. It looked all quiet. Scooter turned to me and put his face close to mine.

"It's only whispers from now on...and then only if you have to."

I nodded and pulled the stocking cap down over my ears. I wished that I had smeared my face with mud or something, like a real night raider.

Scooter reached over the back gate and turned the latch on the inside. The gate swung open as we crawled through and half crawled over to the wood pile. Once behind the pile we were screened from the house and felt a lot safer. Only one pale light glowed from a small window in the back and we were sure that Mr. and Mrs. Tyson must be in the living room listening to the radio or reading or something. Once again Scooter put his face close to mine.

"I'll hand the wood to you and you stack it," he whispered. "Then we'll trade off after while."

Luckily, the wood pile was close to the fence and we didn't have to take more than two or three steps to pile it on the neat row Grandpa Tyson had started. Scooter began handing me the wood and I began stacking it. I was surprised at how fast we could work using this method. Before long we had stacked it as high as the fence and I then began a new row in front of the other.

Everything was going along just fine until suddenly car lights shined up the alley. "Hit the dirt!" I whispered loudly as I dove down behind the wood pile. In one jump, Scooter was by my side.

The car came down the alley slowly and came to a halt by Grandpa Tyson's fence. I slowly raised my head and took a quick look. It was a police car!

I ducked down quickly and whispered to Scooter. "Don't move! It's the cops!"

Scooter looked at me with wide eyes and my heart began thumping like a bass drum. The only thing I could think of was how I was going to explain this to my mom and dad. They would kill me! That is, if I didn't die of a heart attack first!

It seemed as if the whole yard lit up all of a sudden as the spotlight of the police car flashed on and its beam began moving around the yard. Two times it flashed over our heads slowly and then passed to the other side of the yard.

Scooter grabbed my arm and squeezed when we heard the door of the police car door open and close. "Take a look." he whispered.

Lying on the ground, I stretched out and peeked around the side of the wood pile. If I thought my heart was pounding before, it was practically stuck in my throat now as I saw the policeman coming through the back gate with a flashlight. He slowly walked to the back of Grandpa Tyson's garage and shined his light around back there.

"Let's get out of here!" I whispered.

"Right!" whispered Scooter, "I'll go first."

Scooter began crawling on his belly toward the side of Grandpa Tyson's house. I peeked around the woodpile to see where the policeman was. He was just coming around the far corner of the garage when Scooter bumped into a rake leaning against the house. Wouldn't you know it, but the rake slid down and knocked an empty pail off of a small bench. It clattered to the cement sidewalk just as Scooter disappeared around the corner of the house.

"Who's there!" the policeman shouted. "Come out with your hands up!"

My mouth went totally dry as I realized the fix I was in. I was about to be caught by the police or even worse...maybe shot! I didn't dare stand up, but began to shout from behind the woodpile.

"Don't shoot! Don't shoot! I surrender!"

By now the other policeman from the car had joined the first one and they were both walking slowly toward the woodpile. "Come out slowly with your hands over your head!" the policeman called.

I raised my hands over my head and slowly stood up. "This is it." I said to myself, "I'm a goner now."

The policeman shined his flashlight in my face and called out, "Come over here son, and keep your hands up."

Frantically I tried to think of a story I could make up to explain what I was doing here. I was sure they wouldn't believe me if I told them the true story. I had just about reached the policemen when I heard Scooter call from the side of the house.

"One, two, three on Randy! Hiding in the back yard!"

The policeman shined his light toward the house as Scooter came trotting out of the darkness, a surprised look on his face.

"What's going on here officer? Scooter asked as he looked at the policemen and at me.

"You tell us." the policeman answered. "What're you kids doing back here?"

"Well...we're playing hide and go seek." Scooter said in a voice that suggested that anyone would be able to figure out what we were doing.

"Hide and go seek?" he questioned.

I finally found my voice. "Yes sir. I was hiding behind this woodpile and Scooter was it...Did we do something wrong?"

"Well...no," the policeman answered, "But someone called in that a prowler was seen in this backyard...I guess it was you kids playing."

"Yes sir, I'm sure they were mistaken. They probably thought we were burglars or something."

The policeman thought for a moment as he shined the flashlight back and forth between Scooter and me. "O.K.," he finally said, "You kids get out of here. Go home and don't be playing in people's yards anymore."

"Yes sir," we said in unison. "We're sorry if we caused any trouble. We'll go right home."

As the police car drove away I turned to Scooter. "Boy! That was close! I've got to hand it to you Scooter. That was quick thinking."

"Piece of cake." Scooter said rubbing his clenched knuckles against his chest. "Piece of cake."

"Well, let's get out of here before they come back.'

"Wait!" said Scooter holding up his hand. "Let's go back and finish the woodpile. It'll only take us another ten minutes and I'm sure the cops won't be back by then."

"Are you crazy? If they catch us back in there they'll lock us up and throw away the key!"

"Nahh! They won't catch us. Besides, it's more fun when there's a little risk involved."

"I don't know Scooter..." I said beginning to weaken.

"C'mon," he said opening the back gate. "We could have been half done by now."

Looking up I muttered a quick prayer as I followed Scooter back into the yard. By some miracle Grandpa Tyson and his wife hadn't heard the commotion in their back yard and all was quiet. Scooter was right. It only took us another ten minutes and we finished the woodpile. Out in the alley we found a big piece of cardboard, scrawled a big Z on it and went back and propped it against the woodpile.

Stepping back, I looked at it and whispered to Scooter. "Looks good Scooter, now let's get the heck out of here!"

A few moments later we ran out of the alley and turned up the street toward our houses. We stopped at the corner of the next block to say goodnight and go our separate ways. I looked back down the street toward Grandpa Tyson's house. All was quiet in Ghost Lake and the Zorro's had accomplished their first mission.

THE SPY
❉ ❉ ❉

I lay in bed watching the sun come up over the trees outside my window. I thought about what Scooter and I had done the night before and a shudder ran through me when I realized how close we had come to getting into serious trouble. Maybe it would be best if we forgot about the Zorro's and figured out a different kind of club...a safer one, but then I thought of what Grandpa Tyson would say when he found his wood pile done. Maybe we just needed some more planning and practice.

By the time I got to school I felt a little better about it and Scooter reassured me that we'd be more careful next time and wouldn't get caught again as he had thought of a few new wrinkles to add to our next mission.

"What do you mean by new wrinkles, Scooter?" I asked as we walked up the sidewalk to the school.

"I'll tell you at noon hour," he said. "Besides, there are a few more details I have to work out."

I noticed after math class that Scooter was busy writing some kind of a list. Whatever it was, he sure seemed to be concentrating. I was sure that it must be about the Zorros. That was one of the things I liked about Scooter. He was always full of surprises.

Arnold must have suspected something about us also. We didn't know it, but he stole a look at Scooter's list when we went to gym class. I hadn't seen the list yet, but it was enough to tip Arnold off and he was lying in wait when we came out on the playground at noon.

Scooter and I had fallen into a bad habit and Arnold knew about it. Whenever we had something secret to talk about, we went to the far corner of the playground and sat with our backs against the tall, board fence that surrounded the playground. Arnold knew this and had eaten quickly and was lying in hiding behind the fence when we walked across the playground.

I plopped down and rested my back against the fence. "What's up Scooter? What were you writing about this morning?"

Scooter grinned. "Why do you think the cops almost caught us last night?"

"What do you mean?"

"How do you think they knew we were in that yard?"

I had to think about that one for a moment. "Uh... I suppose someone saw us there and called the cops."

"Exactly!" Scooter exclaimed, slamming his fist into his open palm. "And that is the last time anyone is going to see us and report us to anybody!"

"I don't get it."

"Remember that movie we saw a couple of weeks ago? NIGHT RAIDERS? Remember when those commandos sneaked into that town at night and blew up the ammo dump?"

"Yeah? So?"

"We dress like the commandos! We wear black shirts and pants and mud on our faces and hands."

"Hey...neat idea!" I exclaimed. "And we can wear those black stocking caps like they had."

"Right! Good idea!"

"So, what now?" I asked.

"Is that old tree house in your back yard safe to climb up in?"

"Sure. It's only a couple of years old...why?"

"We need a secret place where we can meet after school and make plans for our next raid. It can be kind of a club house for us."

"Yeah, that'll make a good club house. What time?"

"Let's ride by the scene of last night's raid first and see what happened and then we'll split up and look for our next target. We can meet back at the club house at four thirty."

"Sounds good! Let's go." I said as the bell rang, calling us back into school.

As we walked back across the playground, Arnold sneaked out from behind the fence with a sly grin on his face. Slipping into a crowd of kids running for the school, he passed by us undetected.

The afternoon seemed to drag by, but eventually the dismissal bell rang and Scooter and I bolted down the steps two at a time and jumped on our waiting bikes. In another few minutes we turned into Grandpa Tyson's alley and pedaled slowly up to the scene of last night's adventure.

As luck would have it, Grandpa Tyson was just coming out his back gate with a box of wood chips and bark he had raked up from around his wood pile.

"Hello Mr. Tyson," I called as we came to a stop by his gate. "I see you've finished your wood pile. That must have been a lot of work."

"Hello young fellas. Yup, she's all done." He dumped the box of scraps into an empty garbage can and turned to us and scratched his head. "You know boys..." he paused for a moment. "There is something very strange going on."

"What's that Mr. Tyson?" Scooter said with an eager look. "What's so strange?"

"Well..." He began slowly, "I quit piling wood about dark last night and I only had it half piled. When I came out this morning, I'll be darned if the wood pile wasn't finished."

Reaching over his fence he picked up our cardboard and showed it to us. "Here's the real strange part...this here cardboard with this big N on it was leaning against the wood pile."

Scooter and I had all we could do to keep from giggling. I finally managed to ask without laughing. "What do you think it means?"

Grandpa Tyson wrinkled up his nose in thought. "I'm not sure...but I think someone's trying to leave me a message. I suppose they're trying to tell me that they finished my wood pile, but don't want me to know who they are."

Scooter couldn't resist trying to get more information from the old man. "What do you think that mark means?" He asked.

Grandpa Tyson held up the cardboard. "I don't know... what do you think a big N would mean?"

Scooter and I looked at each other in disbelief. He thought it was an N! We had to correct this or the Zorro's were finished.

Reaching for the cardboard, I looked at it carefully, pretending to study it closely. "Uh, I don't think that's an N Mr. Tyson. It looks more like a Z when you hold it this way."

Grandpa Tyson studied the sign. "By golly, I think you're right! It does look more like a Z. Say! Isn't that like that mark that that feller on the radio makes, the mark of the Z?"

"Hey! You're right!" Scooter exclaimed. "That's the mark of Zorro!"

"Yup, that's the one, Zorro." Grandpa Tyson agreed. "What do you suppose...?"

"I don't know," Scooter said. "But it looks like he did you a good deed."

"I reckon he did. Well, anyway, I'm not going to complain about it."

I nodded to Scooter and motioned to go. He took the clue and said to Grandpa Tyson. "Well, it sure was a nice thing that he did for you Mr. Tyson. I wish we could help you track him down but we have to go home for supper. We'll see you."

"All right boys. Thanks for stopping by." He waved and turned back to his yard for another load of chips.

Scooter and I grinned at each other and rode slowly out of the alley and onto the next street. I pulled over to the curb and turned to Scooter. "Boy was that neat! A good deed done and he had no idea how it happened."

"Yeah," said Scooter. "Just like Zorro. Now let's find a target for tonight."

"Right. How about if I go down around the school and up Elm Street? You can cruise down toward Main Street and then up and back to home."

"O.K., I'll meet you at the tree house at four-thirty."

I rode around for about a half an hour but didn't see anything that we could call a target for a good deed. My mind really wasn't on to the task as I was thinking about my tree house and how we could make it into a club house. I hadn't used it much for the last couple of years as I was growing out of those sort of things and besides, before Scooter came, it was not much fun playing alone.

Dad had built if for me when I was in third grade and I played in it a lot that first summer. Dad had used a big Spruce tree growing along our back fence as the base. He dug in three posts for the other support and then tied it all together with boards and a rickety ladder. Only a few boughs of the Spruce tree had been removed, so the remaining boughs served to almost camouflage the tree house. All in all it would serve well for a club house.

True to his word, Scooter knocked on my door at four-thirty. "Find anything?" he asked with a sly smile.

"Nothing. How about you?"

"Does a chicken lay eggs?"

I laughed. Scooter always had some kind of goofy riddle to answer questions. "Let's go up in the tree house," I said.

Once up in the tree house, Scooter peered out the two small windows and asked. "Do you think we're safe up here from spies or other enemies?"

"Of course!" I reassured him. "Who can sneak up on a tree house? Besides, nobody knows we're up here or even cares for that matter."

"O.K., but we can never be too careful. Remember, that's how Zorro has managed to remain a secret for so long. He's always careful and plans ahead."

"Yeah, yeah, so what's the plan?"

Scooter pulled some notes from his pocket. "Do you know of a brown and white house over on Fourth Street?"

"Brown and white...Is it next to a vacant lot on the corner of the block?"

"That's the one."

"I think that's Mrs. Bronson. She lives there all alone."

"I know," Scooter said with a smile. "I checked it all out. She was hanging clothes in her back yard and I just happened to strike up a conversation with her. She was worried about leaving her clothes out all night as she thinks it's going to rain and she has to go and spend the night with her daughter."

"Sounds good," I said. "So, what's the plan?"

"We find some dark clothing, darken our faces, go there after dark, take down her washing, fold it up and put it on her back porch."

"And leave the mark of the Z," I added.

"Right!" exclaimed Scooter. "What do you think?"

"I think it'll work. Did you scout out the area for our approach and escape?"

"Got it!" Scooter said kneeling down over his notes. "Here's a map I drew of the target."

We studied the map for a few moments. It looked simple enough. This was a job that we should have been able to do in fifteen minutes.

"O.K." Scooter said folding up his notes. "I have to go home for supper. We'll use the homework excuse again and meet in front of the school at seven-thirty. It should be dark by then."

We climbed down from the tree house and walked up to the house. "See you at seven-thirty," I said. "I'm going to go in and look for some commando clothes."

Up in the dark boughs of the spruce tree a figure stirred and began slowly climbing down.

THE RAT

❈ ❈ ❈

At seven fifteen the street lights came on. At seven twenty I stepped out the back door, climbed on my bike and began to slowly cruise down toward the school. I pulled over into the shade of a large elm tree about a block from the school and surveyed the situation. I glanced at my watch... seven twenty five. Five minutes to go. I knew Scooter would arrive at precisely seven thirty as this was the way he was, not a minute early or a minute late.

While waiting, I reviewed our plan for tonight's target. I hoped that everything would go as planned and this would be another successful mission for the Zorro's. I shuddered when I thought of how the cops had almost caught us the last time and of how I would have had to explain it to my parents. I was sure they wouldn't have understood what we were trying to do. Right now, I wasn't too sure myself.

At seven twenty nine I pushed out from under the tree and slowly rode toward the school. Just as I predicted, Scooter came riding in from the opposite direction. We didn't say a word but turned and rode silently down the street toward our target. I followed Scooter as he cruised by the front of Mrs. Bronson's house to check if any lights were on. It appeared to be all clear, so we turned at the corner and headed for the alley.

Scooter pulled up to the fence in her back yard and turned with a grin. Pointing at the clothes line he whispered. "There they are...ours for the picking."

We leaned our bikes against the back fence and slipped into the darkened yard. There were four lines of clothes, mostly sheets, pillow cases, and towels.

I poked Scooter in the back. "I'll take these two lines and you take the other two."

Scooter nodded and we began picking the clothes. When my arms were full I whispered to Scooter. "Where can we put these while we pick the rest?"

Scooter motioned with his head toward the back porch of the house. Turning my head I saw three wicker clothes baskets waiting to be filled. I soon deposited my load and went back for another. In a short time the lines were empty and we began folding the dried clothes and putting them in one of the empty baskets.

In fifteen minutes the mission was completed and we set the baskets under the overhang of the porch roof in the event that it might rain. Scooter reached into his back pocket and brought out a piece of paper. As he unfolded it I saw that it was a plain piece of white paper with a big black Z written on it. He then took a clothespin from his pocket and clipped the paper to a sheet on the top of one of the baskets. Turning to me he raised his right hand with his forefinger and thumb encircled to signal mission accomplished.

"O.K. let's get out of here," I said, anxious to leave before we were spotted by someone.

Scooter put his hand on my arm. "Wait! Did you hear something?"

My heart jumped! "No...I don't think so. Did you?"

Scooter turned his head, straining to listen. "I thought I heard something in the yard next door...listen!"

There was total silence except for a dog barking a couple of blocks away. "C'mon," I said. "Let's get out of here!"

Bending low, we trotted out of the yard, jumped on our bikes and rode quietly out of the alley. Two blocks away I finally breathed a sigh of relief. No cops!

We pulled up in front of the school and stopped. "Good job!" Scooter exclaimed. "We were like a well oiled machine! We were in and out of there like cat burglars!"

"Yeah," I agreed. "But we forgot one thing..."

"What was that?"

I laughed. "We forgot to put the mud on our faces!"

Scooter shook his head and laughed. "Oh well... we didn't get caught and we can still do it the next time. This is only the beginning. I see great things in the future for the Zorro's."

"I hope so Scooter, but right now I had better get back home before my folks get suspicious."

"O.K.," Scooter said, pushing off on his bike. "See you in school tomorrow."

I slept well that night, knowing that we had not only accomplished our mission, but that we had helped someone out in doing so. It was a good feeling. Even if nobody ever found out what we had done, I was sure they would have been really proud of us.

The hardest part was talking with my other friends the next morning and not being able to tell of last night's adventure. I was standing on the school steps with a few of the boys when Scooter walked up and winked at me.

"Hey guys! What's new?"

"What's new?" Johnny Tyson asked. "What's ever new in Ghost Lake? This has got to be among the top ten most boring towns in the U.S.A."

"Yeah, I guess you're right," Scooter said with a grin as the school bell rang.

The first inkling of trouble came during math class when Miss Williams asked us to turn in our papers from yesterday. I looked over and saw Scooter paging back and forth through his book and then opening his desk and rummaging around.

Leaning over I whispered. "What's the matter Scooter?"

"I can't find my math paper!" He whispered back with a worried look on his face. "I know I did it. I finished it in class yesterday and put it in my book."

"Maybe it fell out."

"It couldn't have. I never took my book home. It's been here since yesterday."

By this time, Miss Williams had noticed our talking and walked up to Scooter's desk. "What seems to be the problem here boys?"

Scooter had a sick look on his face. "Umm...I can't find my math assignment and I know I finished it and put it in my book."

I looked up at Miss Williams. She had a look on her face that half wanted to believe Scooter and half wanted not to. Two seats down, Arnold was turned around with a smirk on his face. He just loved to see someone else in trouble, especially Scooter and me.

Miss Williams finally spoke. "Well, I'll give you a chance to stay in at noon hour and finish your assignment, but after this, I expect it to be finished on time."

Scooter nodded his head and took out a fresh sheet of paper. I knew he was doing a slow burn, but what other choice did he have?

I assumed that Scooter had probably misplaced his paper and would not have thought anymore about it except that I was the next victim that Lady Luck turned her thumb down on. We were getting ready for lunch and I lifted my desk and opened my pencil box to get my lunch ticket, only to discover that it wasn't there!

I couldn't believe it! I always kept my lunch ticket in there and it had never disappeared before. I leaned over and poked Scooter in the back.

"Scooter...! My lunch ticket is missing."

"What? Your lunch ticket?"

"Yeah, I had it in my pencil box and now it's gone!"

Scooter wrinkled his nose and muttered, "I think I smell a rat!"

"Rat or no rat, I only had three punches off of it and my mom will kill me!"

"Was your name on it?" Scooter asked.

"Sure...I always put my name on it."

"Well, then I wouldn't worry about it. Nobody can use it and it'll probably show up."

"I hope so. Can I borrow a punch from you today?"

"No problem. Let's go eat."

After lunch Scooter headed back to the classroom to finish his math and I went out to the playground. I was soon involved in a softball game and was having a good time until Johnny Tyson nudged me and pointed. "Hey Randy, look over there!"

I looked across the street and my heart stopped. There parked across the street was a black and white police car. Panic began to build in me, but then I calmed myself down, remembering that the mission went well last night. I was sure that the police weren't here looking for me.

By this time several boys had gathered around and began speculating as to why the police were here.

"Maybe there's been a robbery," Bill Hawley suggested.

"Or maybe a murder!" Sam Dawson cried.

Johnny looked at them both with a disgusted look. "Nahh...Nobody ever gets murdered or robbed in Ghost Lake."

At that moment two policemen and a man in a tan suit stepped out of the car and began walking toward the school. As they came opposite the playground they stopped and turned toward us. The man in the tan suit reached in his suit pocket and brought forth a pair of dark sunglasses which he put on and continued scanning the playground. None of them smiled once or said a word and we knew without it being said that these guys meant business.

Sam finally broke the silence as they turned and walked up the steps of the school. "Boy! Does that guy look mean!"

Two minutes later, Shelly Patten came bounding down the school steps and over to our group. "Hey boys! You'll never guess what I just heard in the office!"

"What?" We all said in unison.

"Well, I was in the office buying another lunch ticket when these cops came in and asked for the principal. I wanted to hear what they were saying, so I kind of stood there and pretended I was counting my money."

"Yeah...go on...tell us what you heard!"

Shelly knew she had a captive audience and that we were all dying to hear what secret she had to tell. "The man with the sunglasses did the talking and the other two just stood there looking mean."

"C'mon Shelly!" Johnny cried, grabbing her by the arm. "Spit it out! Why are they here?"

"They're looking for some vandals for destroying property."

With a gulp I asked, "What kind of property?"

Shelly continued, "I guess an old lady left her clothes out on the line last night and some kids tore them down and dragged them around in the mud...From the looks of those police in there I'd say they were dead meat."

The blood drained from my face and a sudden chill came over me. Shelly was right! I already felt like dead meat.

INTERROGATION

✤ ✤ ✤

I wanted to run as far away from there as possible, but couldn't think of where to go. I only had a few moments to decide what to do as the school bell was due to ring at any moment. Deep in my heart I knew I had to go back into the school and that I would probably be blamed for whatever happened. I didn't know if or how they knew, but I just felt that somehow they just knew. Besides, Scooter was still in there and probably didn't have the slightest notion as to what was happening. I had to warn him!

I started toward the school and was almost to the door when the bell rang. Bursting through the door, I half ran down to our classroom and called quickly to Scooter.

"Scooter...Scooter! Quick! Out here!"

We still had five minutes before the final bell and Scooter wanted to finish his math. "Just a minute," he said, "I've only got one more problem."

"You've got a lot more than that!" I exclaimed. "Get out here now!"

Scooter quickly scribbled an answer, grabbed his paper, put it on Miss Williams's desk, and came to the door. Looking at my face he quipped, "What the heck's wrong with you? You look like you've just seen a ghost or something."

"It's worse than that!" I exclaimed. "The cops are here... and I think they're looking for us!"

"Us? Why us?"

"Shelly heard them in the office telling Mr. Kelly that they were looking for some kids that took an old lady's clothes off the line and dragged them around in the mud."

"Well, calm down. You know that it wasn't us. It must have been another old lady. There is more than one in this town, you know."

"I don't know," I said. "I just have a rotten feeling about this. I just know they're looking for us."

"I don't think so," Scooter assured me. "You just feel scared from that other time they almost caught us."

About this time, Shelly Patten came up to us and asked, "What are you boys whispering about?"

"Nothing," I quickly said. "Just boy talk."

Shelly was not about to give up. She lived across the alley from me and had been sticking her nose in my business for years.

"I know you boys are lying. I saw you and Arnold up in your tree house yesterday...I'll bet you have a secret club or something."

"Arnold! Are you nuts?" I exclaimed. "I wouldn't be caught dead in a club with Arnold!"

Scooter squinted at Shelly. "You say you saw Arnold with us in Randy's tree house?"

"You can't fool me, Scooter," She said. "I can even tell you the time because I always leave for my piano lesson at a quarter to five and I stepped out the back door and saw you boys and Arnold climbing down from your tree house."

"We weren't together were we?" I questioned.

"Well, no. You boys were going around the corner of your house when Arnold climbed down."

Scooter looked at me with murder in his eye. "Yeah, well listen Shelly, it's kind of a secret and we'll let you in on it later if you promise not to tell anyone about it. O.K.?"

Shelly thought about it for a second, "Well, O.K., but remember, nothing gets by my eyes and ears."

The final bell rang before Scooter and I could say another word, but thoughts were racing through our minds as we went back into the classroom and took our seats. Of all the dirty, rotten, low down, sneaky, creeps...Arnold had to be at the top of the list. He must have been spying on us from the tree branches or the roof of the tree house. I vowed then and there that I'd get him if it took me the rest of my life.

I quickly forgot about revenge when the door opened and Mr. Kelly, the principal, walked into the room. He bent low over Miss Williams's desk and whispered something to her. Cold sweat once again crept over me. Scooter must have felt the same way as he turned and looked at me with a sick look on his face.

Miss Williams turned toward us and called, "Leonard... Randy, Mr. Kelly would like to visit with you boys for a few minutes."

I let out a long breath of air and slowly stood up and followed Scooter to the door. I was no longer afraid of being caught. I knew I was caught! I resigned myself to the fact and decided that coming clean with the police was the only thing to do.

Mr. Kelly met us at the door and said, "Come with me boys."

I already knew what would be waiting for us, so I was not surprised to see the three policemen seated in Mr. Kelly's office. The uniformed policemen were seated with small notebooks in their laps while the man in the tan suit turned his back to us and stared out the window. None of them spoke a word as we came into the office.

Mr. Kelly motioned to two chairs by his desk. "Sit here boys."

We sat with folded hands, not knowing whether we should say anything or not. We decided not to. I began to feel a cold chill on the back of my neck and my stomach felt sick. I glanced over at Scooter and I could tell he was feeling the same way. For thirty seconds the two police-men stared at us while the man at the window continued looking out. When he slowly turned and looked at us I realized that this was big time trouble!

Even in the principal's office, he still had the sunglass-es on. They were so dark that you couldn't see his eyes. A toothpick protruded from his lower lip and he chewed slowly on it as he studied us sitting there before him.

Finally he pointed at me and said, "Name."

"Randy...Uh...Randy Bigsley," I stammered.

Not saying another word, he swung his finger over at Scooter.

"Leonard...Leonard Dobson," Scooter said, his voice breaking with fear.

One of the uniformed policemen wrote the information down as we spoke. The other sat there like stone.

Mr. Tan Suit continued swinging his finger back and forth at us and in one word commands had us tell our age, address, phone number and parent's names. It was evident that we were going to have a police record, which wasn't a very comforting thought.

Having gotten all the necessary information, he turned to us with a sneer and said, "Okay boys, we can do this the hard way or the easy way... and if I were you, I'd take the easy way."

"I...I'm not sure what you mean sir," I said.

He reached in a manila folder, withdrew my lunch ticket and placed it near me on Mr. Kelly's desk. "Do you know a Mrs. Bronson?" he asked.

"Yes sir."

He reached into the folder again, withdrew Scooter's math paper and placed it by my lunch ticket. Turning to Scooter, he asked, "Do you know a Mrs. Bronson?"

By this time, Scooter seeing the lunch ticket and math paper, had put two and two together and regained his composure. "Yes we know Mrs. Bronson and I think I know why you're here. I would like to explain what happened...or what I think happened."

"Go on," Mr. Tan Suit said.

"One of the kids overheard you telling why you're here and they said it was because some kids tore down Mrs. Bronson's wash off the line and dragged it through the mud."

"That's right, and we have reason to believe that it was you two boys that did it. So...why don't you come clean and confess."

"Excuse me sir," Scooter continued. "I consider myself somewhat of an amateur detective and I'd like to present a scenario as to what I think happened."

Wow! I didn't think Scooter knew any of those big words, but I wasn't going to argue at that time. I decided to let him carry the ball for awhile and see what happened.

"This better be good," Mr. Tan Suit muttered.

Scooter went on, "Well, first of all let's imagine that Randy and I did do it. Do you think we'd be careless enough to leave our lunch ticket and math paper at the scene? I mean, I could see one of us possibly losing a piece of paper at the scene, but both of us? And isn't it a coincidence that the evidence just happens to have our names on it?"

"Hmmmm...," Mr. Tan Suit pondered. "What you say makes sense, but it seems that you know a little too much of what happened, and there is one small item that you have overlooked."

"What's that sir?" Scooter asked.

"Mrs. Bronson told us of a boy who visited over the fence with her yesterday afternoon. He asked a lot of questions and her description fits you perfectly."

We had forgotten about that! Mrs. Bronson had seen Scooter and would be able to identify him! I could see that things didn't look good for us and our only way out was to break the secret oath of the Zorro's and tell all.

"Aahhh...sir?" I began. "I think I can explain why things appear to be what they are, but if I could start at the beginning I think it would clear up a lot of things."

Mr. Tan Suit stared at me with no eyes. "Go ahead...Bill, take this down."

The younger policeman opened his notebook and clicked his pen. "Go slow," he ordered.

I began with how we had wanted to start a secret club and had hit upon the idea of the Zorro's. I explained that the purpose of our club was to do only good deeds and to do it in secret, keeping our identity unknown. I told of how we had piled Grandpa Tyson's woodpile and left the mark of the Z.

At that point, the policeman named Bill interrupted me by exclaiming, "That's where I've seen you before! I've been trying to place you and now I remember. You were in the old man's back yard playing hide and go seek!"

"No," I corrected him. "We were really piling wood. That was our first good deed target and Mrs. Bronson was to be our second. We picked her clothes for her, folded them and placed them in her clothes basket on her back porch. When we left her yard last night the clothes were clean and dry."

"Then how do you explain what happened?" Mr. Tan Suit asked.

Scooter jumped in. "We were framed! That's what happened and I'll bet a million bucks I know who did it!"

"Wait a minute!" I cautioned. "We have a good idea who it was, but we can't prove it. If he were questioned he'd deny it and you'd never be able to prove anything."

"So what do you suggest?" Mr. Tan Suit said.

Scooter looked at me with a grin. "How do you catch a rat?"

"A trap!" I exclaimed.

INSPECTOR 4

✤ ✤ ✤

Mr. Tan Suit glanced over at the other two policemen and then back to us. "O.K.," he finally said. "I'll give you ten days to clear yourselves. If you haven't come up with anything by then, I'm going to come over and have a little visit with your parents. Is that understood?"

"Yes sir!" I said with relief. "But, may I ask a question?"

"What is it?"

"Could I please have your name and phone number?" I asked. "We may need some help from you and I'd like to know where I can get in touch with you."

"I don't give my name out to anyone," Mr. Tan Suit said in a cold voice. "If you want to contact me, just call the police station and tell them you have a message for Inspector 4. I'll get back to you."

Scooter and I looked at each other with wide eyes. Inspector 4! It had to be a code name! What a name! This was going to be better than I thought.

Inspector 4 went on, "If I don't hear from you boys in a week, I'll find you to determine what's happening."

"Yes sir," I said. "We won't say anything to the other kids about this. Besides, we don't want to tip off the real culprit as to what is happening."

Inspector 4 smiled a sinister smile, "Maybe we do, son, maybe we do. You see, if you boys are telling the truth, someone is enjoying seeing you get into trouble. Maybe we should let him think that this is exactly what's happening and he'll let his guard down some more."

"Hey! That's right!" Scooter exclaimed. "If Ar..., I mean if he thinks we're in big trouble he'll be ripe for the picking."

"That's right," Inspector 4 said. "Is the suspect in the same class as you boys?"

"Yes sir."

"Do you go outside for your gym class this afternoon?"

"Yes sir."

"O.K., Here's the plan..."

Five minutes later Mr. Kelly escorted us back to our classroom. You could have heard a pin drop as we slowly walked back to our seats. I could just about imagine what each kid in the room was thinking. None of them would have traded places with us for all the money in the world. I could especially imagine what Arnold was thinking. He was probably happier than ever, thinking that we were in trouble and that he was the main reason for it.

A couple of kids tried to whisper questions to us, but Miss Williams reminded them that we were still having class and they were to be quiet. I had the feeling that even Miss Williams felt a little sorry for us. I assumed that Mr. Kelly had told her why we were being asked to go to the office and I had the feeling that she didn't believe that Scooter and I would have anything to do with vandalism. At least I was hoping that she felt that way.

Scooter and I managed to appear to be absorbed in our class work, but as the time drew near to go outdoors for recess; Scooter turned and gave me a wink. I quickly winked back and half smiled in anticipation of the next class period.

At last, Miss Williams stood up by her desk and announced, "Alright class, we'll go outside for our afternoon recess. We'll play softball and we will have the same teams as yesterday."

A few moans and complaints arose from the losers of yesterday's game, but for the most part, that was forgotten and everyone was anxious to hear what Scooter and I had to say.

"Did you guys have to talk to the cops?" Barry Thomas whispered as we lined up.

I noticed that Arnold had lined up behind us and was listening carefully to what was being said. Scooter saw him also and threw him the first piece of bait.

"Yeah," Scooter said in his tough guy voice. "But they weren't able to pin anything on us. I think that's the last we'll see of them."

"Was it about that deal we heard about at Mrs. Bronson's house?" Sam asked.

"Well..." I hesitated. "We're really not supposed to talk to anyone about anything."

With that, everyone seemed impressed with the seriousness of it all. But of course Arnold couldn't keep his big mouth shut.

"All I can say is that you guys must have been pretty stupid in whatever you did. It didn't take the cops long to find you."

"We're not in jail yet, Arnold," Scooter shot back.

"No, but you're not exactly jumping for joy either," he said with a grin.

Out on the playground we quickly took to the softball field. Scooter and I tried to keep our minds on the game, but it was very difficult, especially when we knew what was about to happen.

Each team had batted twice and our team was just coming in from the field when the black and white police car slowly drove by the playground. Every kid out there had their eyes glued on it as it turned the corner and came to a stop by the ball diamond. Scooter and I looked around the ball field nervously as if looking for an escape route.

Even Miss William's mouth dropped when the back door of the police car opened and Inspector 4 stepped out. He still had his sunglasses on and a fresh toothpick drooped from his lip. He didn't say a word, but took two steps to the sidewalk, pointed at Scooter and me, and motioned to the open car door.

Scooter and I handed our gloves to a couple of the boys and with hanging heads, walked slowly to the car. As Inspector 4 held the door, we stopped for one moment and looked back at the class. It was working! Even Arnold had a scared look on his face. Inspector 4 stepped into the back seat with us, closed the door, and the police car drove off. Miss Williams was the only one on the field that knew we wouldn't be seen for the rest of the day.

About four blocks away the police car pulled over and Inspector 4 stepped out. "Here's where you get out boys. Make sure you don't get home any earlier than usual. We don't want to worry your parents. Remember, you have ten days to clear this up. I'll check with you in a week to see how things are coming."

"Thank you sir!" We said in unison. "Thank you very much!"

As the police car drove away, Scooter and I sat down on the boulevard with our backs to a big Oak tree. "I don't know Scooter...," I said. "I can't believe everything that's happened today."

"And how!" Scooter exclaimed. "I thought I'd die when we walked into Mr. Kelly's office and saw that guy standing by the window."

"He is a scary looking character, isn't he?"

"I didn't know Ghost Lake had a detective on the police department." Scooter said.

"Me neither. I've never seen him around before."

"Maybe they brought him in special on this case."

"I don't know...you wouldn't think that this case would be such a big deal."

"Well anyway, we have to figure something out to get ourselves out of this and nail the real culprit."

"I'm sure it was Arnold," I said. "But first we have to find out for sure."

"Yeah, let's meet at your place after school, and not in the tree house. Up in your room where we'll be safe."

"O.K., how about five o'clock?"

"Five o'clock," Scooter said. "Now...let's walk slowly home."

Scooter arrived at my house at five o'clock, right on the dot as usual. We quickly went up to my room and closed the door. Trusting nobody, I looked out the window, checked my closet and then looked under the bed.

"It's safe," I declared. "Where do we start?"

"Do you have a sheet of paper and a pencil?" Scooter asked.

I dug in my desk drawer and brought forth a pencil and paper. "Why do you want these?"

"I want to make some notes on what happened today and work backwards from there. That way I think we can figure out what went wrong."

It sounded logical, but actually, I think Scooter wanted to act like the police. You know, taking notes and stuff.

But hey, who was I to argue with his methods if they got us out of the trouble we were in.

"O.K.," Scooter said. "Ask a question."

"What?"

"Ask a question...What don't we know?"

I thought about that for a few moments and then said, "If it was Arnold, why did he drag the clothes through the mud?"

Scooter gave me a disgusting look. "That's a pretty obvious question and answer," he said. "He did it to get us in trouble!"

"Yeah, I guess you're right. What questions do you have?"

Scooter wrote some notes down on the paper and then studied them for a minute. Leaning back in his chair he studied the ceiling and tapped the pencil on his teeth.

"O.K.," he began. "We know, based on what Shelly told us, that Arnold most likely heard everything we said in the tree house. The question I have is...How did Arnold know that we were going to meet in the tree house at four-thirty?"

"That's right! How in the world did he know that?" Let's go back some more," I suggested. "When did we make the plans to meet in the tree house?"

"Good question! Let's see...We made the plans at noon hour...out on the playground."

"Right! We were sitting in the corner of the playground, up against the fence!"

Scooter slapped his knee. "And I'll bet you fifty bucks that Arnold was behind that fence!"

"How do we know that for sure?" I asked.

"We don't. That's the problem."

"How about..." I said with a grin. "If we feed him a little more bait and see if he takes it?"

Scooter smiled. I could see the wheels turning already. "Is there anyone in our class you can trust, after me of course?"

"Let's see...I think Shelly would be one. Arnold is always mean to her and I'm sure she'd love to get back at him.

"A girl?" Scooter questioned. "I don't know about letting a girl in on this."

"She's perfect." I argued. "Shelly's a tomboy...she hates Arnold and she's always sticking her nose in where it doesn't belong. I've known her since kindergarten and we've been friends all along. She can keep a secret and nobody would suspect her."

"Well...if you say so, I guess we can include her. We may need her help tomorrow. She can keep an eye on Arnold while we lay out the bait."

SHELLY THE SPOOK

❖ ❖ ❖

Scooter and I walked to school together the next morning and finalized our plan along the way. Scooter had named this plan "**Operation Rat bait**" and by this afternoon we would know if Arnold had spied on us the other day. We found Shelly Patten right away and got her off to the side alone.

"Shelly," I asked, "I've got a big favor to ask you."

Shelly looked at us with a wrinkled nose. "Does this have anything to do with what happened with the cops yesterday?"

"Well...kind of," I said, "But it's nothing that will get you into any kind of trouble or anything. Besides, we're not really supposed to talk to anyone about what happened yesterday."

"Well, what is it?" She asked.

Scooter cupped his hand to Shelly's ear and whispered, "It's kind of like being a private eye...All you have to do is keep an eye on Arnold during noon recess and report back to us everything he does."

"That's all?"

"Yes, except that you can't let Arnold know that you're watching him."

"I can do that. It'll be fun. But I wish you boys could tell me more about what's going on."

"In time Shelly, in time," I assured her. "When this is all over we'll tell you the whole thing and you'll see what an important part you're playing in this thing. I picked you because I trust you more than any other kid in sixth grade."

Shelly blushed. "Well, thanks Randy. I won't let you down. That creep Arnold won't be able to blink without me knowing about it."

"That's great, Shelly! I knew we could count on you. Now, we don't want to be seen with you for now. We don't want Arnold to become suspicious."

"Right." Shelly said as the morning bell rang. "I'll have a full report ready for you right after recess."

"O.K. we'll see you then." we said as we went our own way and up the steps of the school.

Even with the trouble we were in, it was kind of fun to walk into that classroom that morning and have every pair of eyes on us. It was almost as good as having your leg in a cast and having to wear crutches. Besides, I knew we didn't drag the clothes through the mud and I was confident that the truth would win out in the end...I hoped.

Miss Williams tried to carry on with class as if nothing had happened, but I noticed the other kids sneaking a peek at Scooter and me every once in a while. I knew they were dying to know what happened and I would have dearly loved to be able to tell them every gruesome detail, but it would have to wait.

Arnold was especially antsy this morning and I figured that he, more than anyone, was trying to find out what had happened. I was sure he was more interested in what was going to happen to us and was more than likely trying to find a way to push us over the edge and get us into more trouble.

As we lined up for our mid-morning bathroom break, I threw Arnold the first piece of bait. As Scooter and I lined up behind him, I leaned over to Scooter and said in a loud whisper, "Something's come up. We need to talk at noon hour."

Scooter turned to me with a wink. "Right, same place?"

"Same place," I said in a little louder whisper.

Noon hour finally came and we all went down to the cafeteria. About half of the class wanted to know what happened yesterday. Most of them wanted to know where the cops took us and how long they held us. We told them that we weren't supposed to talk about any of that or we could get into more trouble. They accepted that and it even made us more important as it seemed that we were involved in a major crime of some sort. Someone asked the question as to what it was like to ride in a police car and this was one thing we could talk about.

Scooter took over on this question and played it to the hilt. "That was some experience!" he began. "We were in the backseat with the detective with the sunglasses and they had this wire cage built between the front and back seats. I guess that's so we couldn't hit or club the cops in the front seat when they weren't looking. They also didn't have any door handles on the inside of the back seat. That's so you can't jump out and escape."

"Did they have any guns or anything?" Sam asked.

"Oh yeah, they had guns alright! Each cop had a pistol and they had a sawed off shotgun in a rack on the ceiling over the front seat. No way would I mess with them...they mean business!"

These answers seemed to satisfy most of the kids and I could see the envy in their eyes at the attention that Scooter and I were getting. Finally I nodded to Scooter, signaling that it was time to go and put our second phase of "**Operation Rat bait**" into place.

As we walked out onto the playground I glanced around and sure enough, Arnold was coming out the door of the school and watching us. I nudged Scooter, "Don't look now but the rat is about to take the bait."

Scooter kept on walking, speaking out of the side of his mouth. "Let's head straight for the corner of the fence."

We turned around and sat down as we reached the corner of the fence. Arnold was no longer in sight. I leaned over and whispered to Scooter, "Let's wait a minute to give him time to sneak around."

Scooter nodded and held up three fingers, signaling phase three of "**Operation Rat bait**."

I pressed my ear to the fence and in a moment heard a slight scuffle from the other side. I nodded and winked at Scooter. He grinned back at me.

"So what's come up?" he began.

I turned my head more toward the fence. "I think the story is out about what happened. I've heard some of the kids talking about it and a few have asked questions."

"Big deal!" Scooter said with confidence. "We know we didn't do anything wrong and that's what counts."

"Not really...If the rest of the class believes that we actually did it, then nobody will trust us again and they'll all think we're a couple of hoods."

"Yeah," Scooter answered, turning his head toward the fence. "I see what you mean. This could affect us for the rest of our school years. The coaches won't want us on their teams and girls won't want to go out with us and their parents wouldn't let them anyway, even if they wanted to."

"And teachers might give us poor grades because of our bad reputation," I added.

"Have you got any ideas about how we can clear this thing up and save ourselves?" Scooter asked with a wink.

This was the signal to feed Arnold the next chunk of bait. We didn't want him to know that we suspected him of being involved in any way.

"Well," I began, "The way I got it figured is that it must have been a pure accident the way things happened. I'd bet anything that a couple of stray dogs got at those clothes and dragged them around the yard. We should have been more careful about putting them up out of the reach of any animals."

"Yeah," Scooter answered, holding back a giggle, "Next time we'll have to be more careful...if there is a next time."

"There has to be!" I exclaimed. "That's the only way we can prove that we were trying to do a good deed. Our next target has to be something spectacular so we can come out as heroes!"

"Hey! That'll be great!" Scooter cried. "We'll be the envy of every kid in the class and Arnold and his Skulls can go eat rocks!"

Scooter was laying it on a little thick and I cringed a little when he said that about Arnold. If this didn't work out, Arnold would never let us forget it and our reputations really would be ruined.

"So...what should we do for our next target?" I asked.

"I don't know..." Scooter said, "It'll take some thinking and planning. Let's see...tomorrow is Saturday and I have some chores to do in the morning. In the meantime, let's both be thinking of a new target and meet in the tree house tomorrow afternoon."

"Sounds good," I said, pointing at the fence. "What time should we meet?"

Scooter caught my drift and nodded his head. "Oh...how about right after lunch, say one o'clock."

"One o'clock it is...at the tree house." I said very clearly.

"Let's go," Scooter concluded. "The bell is about to ring."

We got up and walked slowly back across the playground. Shelly was waiting for us on the steps of the school. She was really playing the private eye part as she looked both ways, and then signaled us over to the side of the steps.

"What's the report Shelly?" I asked.

Shelly lowered her voice and talked out of the side of her mouth. "As soon as I saw you boys start across the playground I observed Arnold wander over to the edge of the fence where it goes around the playground. He then stood there until you boys reached the corner of the fence and sat down. At this point he took off running around behind the fence. I quickly followed him at a distance so he couldn't see me and when he turned the corner of the fence I ran up there and peeked around the corner. At this time he slowed down and kind of sneaked along the fence until he reached the place where you boys were sitting. He then crawled right up to the fence and put his ear to it. He stayed there all the time you were there and when you got up to leave he sneaked out of there and ran out on the playground. He's out there now with Bird legs and Grogan right now."

"And I'll bet he's giving them an earful too!" Scooter added.

"So what's my next assignment?" Shelly asked. "Can you tell me any more now?"

"No, I'm sorry we can't Shelly," I said. "But you did a great job and we can still use your help if you want to help"

"You bet!" Shelly exclaimed. "That was fun! What else do you need?"

"We'd kind of like you to keep doing what you did. Watch Arnold. If you can overhear some of his conversation or plans, it would help us a lot."

"You've got it! I'll be like a ghost...Arnold won't even know I'm there. Just call me Shelly the Spook."

Shelly didn't know it, but she had just given herself a nickname. From that day on she was known as Shelly the Spook, or just plain Spook.

HACKSAW HENDERSON

❖ ❖ ❖

Scooter and I walked home from school together. There were still a few things in my mind that weren't real clear. Now we had set the bait, but I had no idea as to what we would use for a trap.

"Do you really have chores to do tomorrow?" I asked Scooter.

"Nah...I just said that so Arnold won't come sneaking around tomorrow morning and spying on us. We need some time to come up with another target. This has to be a good one because we have to trap the Rat at the same time."

"I was thinking, Scooter, we should come up with some code names for us, in case we need to send messages when we don't want anyone to know who it is."

"Good idea! Remember that war movie we saw last week. They used code names like Fireball one and Red Dog? We could come up with some names like that!"

"Yeah...lets see...I think I'll be...I know! I'll be Black Bat Leader! How about it?"

"Sounds great!" Scooter exclaimed. "And...I'll be...hmm...I think I'll be Eagle One. What do you think?"

"Great! We'll use those names when we call on the phone or send notes and stuff."

We walked for a moment in silence, lost in our thoughts of what happened today.

Finally I spoke up. "Why don't you spend the night at my house tonight? I'll ask my mom if you can stay over and you can go home, ask your mom and call me. That way we can get started on planning for the next target."

"Sounds good," Scooter said. "I don't see any problem with that. Maybe we can even go out tonight and look for a target."

"Yeah, it may take awhile to find something that will fit in with what we need."

"Hmmm..." Scooter said thoughtfully. "I never thought much about that. Maybe we should think of what we want to do before we pick a target."

"That's simple...We want to get the cops off of our backs and onto Arnold's."

"Right! And if we can arrange for Arnold to get caught in the act, then he won't be able to squirm out from under it."

We reached the corner where we parted and paused for a moment.

"I'll ask my mom and call you right away," Scooter said.

"O.K. Eagle One...Remember the code."

"Yeah, and I was thinking. We should also have a code name for our plan...How about **Operation Rat Trap**?"

"Perfect! I'll see you in about an hour or so."

I thought about what had happened today as I walked the rest of the way home by myself. It was kind of nice to have Shelly in with us. We used to be the best of friends in first and second grade. We even walked to school together back then, but as we grew older we kind of grew away from each other. She seemed to enjoy helping us, but I didn't want her to get into trouble, so we would have to be careful. I didn't like the idea that we had gotten into trouble, but it was still fun to be spying and using code names and planning for our next target. Everything had to go right this time. If we got caught again we'd be dead ducks.

I wasn't home fifteen minutes when the phone rang. I figured it must be Scooter so I yelled, "I've got it!" and ran to pick it up.

I put the phone to my ear and took a chance that it must be Scooter on the other end. "Black Bat Leader," I said softly into the phone.

"Eagle One to Black Bat Leader...the coast is clear. Will arrive at seventeen hundred hours."

I didn't want Scooter to know that I didn't know what Seventeen hundred hours meant, so I just said, "Roger Eagle One...Black Bat Leader out."

I went up to my room to change my school clothes and read some comics while I was waiting for Scooter. I was hoping that he would come up with some ideas for the next target because I was fresh out of ideas. I was even beginning to have some doubts about how far we were carrying this thing. It was fun and all, but I was worried that we might get ourselves into more trouble. Inspector 4 was always on the back of my mind and I knew we only had eight days left to clear our names.

When Scooter arrived my worries passed. He had a way of looking on the bright side of things and didn't seem to worry about anything. I didn't even know he had come yet. I just looked up from my comic and there he was standing in the doorway with a big grin on his face and a paper bag under his arm. I jumped a little as I saw him, as I had never heard a footstep.

"Gee Scooter; do you have to sneak in like that? You about scared the liver out of me."

"Just practicing, Black Bat...just practicing," he said placing the bag on a chair. "By the way, didn't you tell your mom I was coming?"

I slapped my forehead. "I completely forgot! Why? Did she say anything about it?"

"Not really. She was just wondering what I was doing here and asked if my mom knew about it."

"What's in the bag?" I said changing the subject.

Scooter closed the door, picked up the bag, and brought it over to my bed. Reaching in, he began pulling out items. "These, my friend, are the tools of any good spy. Binoculars, camouflage head net, army flashlight, knife, and compass."

"Where'd you get them and why do we need them?"

"I got them from my uncle, the one who gave me the pup tent. He has a lot of this army surplus stuff and I figured since we were into codes and spying that this stuff would come in handy...and guess what else?"

"You don't have a gun in that bag, I hope."

Scooter laughed. "No,...it's something better. I think I found our target for Operation Rat Trap and if I'm not mistaken, it's a doozy."

"You're kidding! How'd you find a target so soon?"

"Well, I'm not completely sure yet. We'll have to check it out in the morning. Do you know an old man by the name of Henderson?"

"I hope you don't mean Hacksaw Henderson." I shuddered.

"Who's Hacksaw Henderson?" Scooter said with a frown.

"He's a mean old goat that lives out on Mill Pond Road. You see him around in the fall selling apples."

"That's the guy!" Scooter exclaimed. "He was just over at my mom's selling her some apples."

"Oh no, Scooter! I'm not messing with that guy. Do you know how he got his name, Hacksaw?"

"I suppose he murdered his wife with a hacksaw or some dumb thing like that."

"No, but just about as bad. A couple of years ago Arnold and some kids sneaked out to his place and were stealing apples. They were up in his tree when he came out of the house and saw them. They bailed out of the tree and ran in the woods with old man Henderson right behind them. He kept yelling that when he caught them he was going to cut off their hands with a hacksaw. Luckily they got away, but no kid has gone near that place since and I am not about to be the first."

"Gee, I thought he was a nice old man. I visited with him for a while and he never said anything mean. Besides, he could use some help from the Zorros."

"You talked to Hacksaw Henderson?" I said in disbelief.

"Of course I talked to him! He was at my house selling apples. My mom bought half a bushel from him and he said that was all he was going to have left because he hurt his leg this summer and can't climb a ladder anymore. He said there were a lot more apples up in his tree, but he can't reach any more from the ground."

"And you want the Zorros to sneak in there, pick his apples for him, and get our hands cut off with a hacksaw?"

"Ahhh!...I don't believe that! Sure, he probably said that, but I can't believe that he'd ever do anything like that. I'm sure he was only saying that to scare those kids from coming back."

I knew I wasn't going to change Scooter's mind that easy so I figured I might just as well listen to his plan. It wouldn't hurt to listen, or so I thought.

"So...How do you propose to do this suicide mission?" I asked.

"Well I thought we could ride out to his place in the morning and kind of just visit with him. At the same time we could look over the situation and draw up the best plan of attack."

"Uhh...I don't know if that would be such a good idea. I mean, what if he doesn't like us hanging around his place or something?"

"He won't mind! I'm telling you...he's a nice guy!"

Scooter had once again talked me into it. I imagined that if we went to Hacksaw's house in the daylight it wouldn't be too bad. Maybe this was one of Scooter's ideas that might work.

The rest of the evening we spent in complete freedom of school, the Zorros, and our problem with the police. After supper we cruised around town on our bikes and then came back and had popcorn and apple cider. Up in my room we invented a new game called Stalag 17, based on a movie we had seen about a prisoner of war camp. One of us would go out in the hall while the other was hiding my little plastic soldiers in different places around the room. The rule was that they had to be somewhere in the open where you could see them, but the trick was that the room was completely dark and you had to use a flashlight like a searchlight from the prisoner of war camp. We also had to stay in one place and we picked my bed as being the guard tower with the searchlight. When a soldier was spotted in the light, the spotter said "Halt!", and the other of us would go and pick up the soldier. The object of the game was to see who could find the most soldiers in three minutes.

We played this game until about ten o'clock and finally called it quits when Scooter tied me with twelve soldiers in three minutes. We turned in and read comics in bed for another half hour before turning out the light. My eyes were growing heavy when Scooter broke the silence once again.

"Let's get an early start tomorrow. I'd like to get a good look at the Henderson place before we talk to him."

"Good idea Scooter...Good idea. Now, let's get some sleep."

SCOUTING OUT

❖ ❖ ❖

The next morning dawned bright and sunny. It was going to be one of those beautiful early autumn days. The leaves were just beginning to turn and there was a hint of coolness in the air.

Scooter and I were up by eight o'clock, had a good breakfast and were on the road by nine. Scooter had rigged up a little packsack in which he carried his binoculars, knife, and camouflage head nets. He said that a spy must always be prepared and he didn't want to ride all the way back into town to get his stuff in case he needed it. I didn't argue with him.

We knew we had a lot of work to do. We had to case out the Henderson place, come up with a plan, and be back at the tree house at one o'clock. We felt for sure that Arnold would be up in the tree hiding and we didn't want to be late. He might get bored and leave without hearing our plan.

"Lead the way," Scooter said as we hopped on our bikes and started down the street. "You know where it is, don't you?"

"Yeah, it's only a little way out of town. We'll be there in ten minutes."

Mill Pond Road was all gravel and we had to eat the dust of a couple of cars as we pedaled around the edge of Mill Pond and began the long climb up Taylor's Hill. The Henderson place was over the hill and down in a little valley on the other side.

"Let's rest a minute," Scooter puffed as we reached the top of Taylor's Hill. "How much farther is it?

"It's just down the hill and around the curve," I said, matching Scooter puff for puff. "That's quite a climb isn't it?"

"You can say that again! At least we can coast down on the way back. Let's go."

The hill wasn't so steep on the other side and the morning breeze coming off of the Mill Pond cooled us as we coasted slowly down the other side. Rounding the curve we spied the Henderson place nestled at the bottom of another small hill.

"There it is!" I called, pointing down the road.

"Pull over," Scooter said. "I want to check this out.

We pulled over to the side and put our kick stands down. Scooter took off his packsack and pulled out the binoculars.

He scrambled up the bank along the road and lay on his belly, studying the Henderson place through his binoculars.

After a minute I called up to him. "What do you see?"

Scooter never took his eyes away from the binoculars, but waved his arm for me to join him. I climbed up the sand bank and lay down beside him.

Scooter didn't put the binoculars down, but gave me a running commentary of what he saw. "As I make it out there's a house, a barn of some sort and a couple of small sheds.

Yup, I think the Zorro's could take this place with no problem."

"Let me see," I said reaching for the binoculars.

Scooter handed them to me and I put them up to my eyes and began turning the little wheel in the middle to focus them to my eyes. Scooter was right. There wasn't a whole lot to the Henderson place. Just a few buildings and some chickens and two pigs rooting around behind a small shed.

"That big tree must be the apple tree," I observed. "It's the only decent sized tree in the yard."

Scooter stood up and brushed off his pants. "Well, let's go down there and ask old Hacksaw if he's murdered any kids lately."

"Very funny." I said as I stood up and looked from another angle.

"C'mon," Scooter said. "We don't have all day you know."

Scooter put the binoculars back in the packsack and then hid it behind a bush along the road. We didn't want the old man to see it and start questioning us about it. In another minute we were coasting up the Henderson driveway. There was no turning back now.

The old man stepped out of the house as we got off of our bikes and parked them along his fence. Hacksaw Henderson didn't look as bad to me as I had imagined. His snow white hair was neatly combed and he wore a pair of faded bib overalls. From across the yard he kind of reminded me of Gramps. Maybe Scooter was right.

"Good morning Mr. Henderson!" Scooter called as we walked up to the house. "Remember me, Scooter Dobson? You sold some apples to my mom yesterday afternoon."

"Oh yes...hello young man. What brings you out here? Were the apples alright?"

Scooter tipped his head toward me and said, "The apples were great. In fact my mom is home baking an apple pie right now. This is my friend Randy Bigsley and we were just out riding our bikes and we thought we'd stop in and say hello. This is a real nice place you've got here."

"Well thank you. We've lived here for forty years," Mr. Henderson said. "We like it. It's nice and peaceful most of the time."

It was kind of an awkward moment. Scooter and I had not rehearsed what we were going to say and I wasn't sure which way the conversation was going to go. Scooter as usual was thinking on his feet and steered the conversation in the direction he wanted.

"Is that your apple tree over there?" he said pointing.

"Yup, c'mon over and I'll see if I can't knock down a couple of juicy ones for you boys."

I couldn't believe it! Scooter was right! The old man was actually nice. He walked over and picked up a long pole by the shed and pushed the end of it up into the apple tree. With a few short swings several apples tumbled down through the branches and bounced at our feet.

"I used to be able to go up on a ladder and pick this tree clean," he said. "But I banged up my knee this summer and I can't climb anymore. So, I guess I'll just have to forget about those up near the top for this year."

"We could help you!" Scooter blurted out.

I looked at Scooter in disbelief! What was he doing? This was going to be our target for operation Rat Trap and here he was volunteering our services! I slyly gave him a poke in the ribs with my elbow to shut him up.

Scooter looked at me with a smile that indicated he knew what he was doing. Anyway it was too late. He had already said we would help.

Mr. Henderson thought about that for a moment. "Well... maybe you could. I was planning on hiring some help for some other things I have to do, but maybe you two boys would be just the ticket."

I decided to play along with Skinny, hoping he knew what he was doing. "Sure," I said. "We'll help you. What other kind of projects do you have?"

"I've been thinking of tearing down that old pig shed," he said pointing to the rickety shed over by the apple tree.

"It's been there for as long as I've lived here and it's about to fall down."

What about the pigs?" Scooter asked. "Where will they live?"

Mr. Henderson pointed at a newer shed beyond the old one. "I've built a newer shed and have moved the pigs over to it just last week. They'll be warmer in there and have more room to move around."

Scooter started walking over toward the shed, "I think we could tear this down. Do you want the boards taken off carefully or can it just be knocked down?"

"I don't care how it comes down," Mr. Henderson said. "It ain't worth nothing except maybe kindling wood, but there is one problem."

"What's that?" I asked.

Mr. Henderson pointed to a small hole in the ground under the side wall. "It seems an old skunk has made his home under the floor, and until I can trap him out of there, I don't want to be fooling around tearing the place down."

"Hmmm..." said Scooter. "Perfect."

I glanced at Scooter and he had that look in his eyes. I knew the wheels were turning again and I was beginning to read his mind.

"How do you figure on trapping him?" Scooter asked. "I mean without him stinking up the place."

"I have a live trap that's just big enough for him to crawl into. When the doors fall down it pushes his tail down and he can't lift it. If a skunk can't lift his tail, he can't release his scent. I'll just pick up the trap and take him down the road a few miles and turn him loose."

"Are you sure it'll work?" I asked.

"Oh sure, I've done it lots of times."

Scooter smiled his evil smile again. "When are you going to set the trap?"

"I'll do it right now. The sooner I get him out of here, the sooner you boys can report for work. How does that sound?"

"When do you think we can start?" Scooter asked.

"Well...let's see. My wife and I have to be gone all day tomorrow and we won't be back till late tomorrow night, so this weekend is out. Besides, I should clean it out before we tear it down. There must be a foot of wet, sloppy, manure in there. If I can catch the skunk tonight and clean out the manure on Monday...I suppose next Saturday would be a good time to tear it down."

"Next Saturday would be great!" Scooter exclaimed. "Now, what about the apples? Show us where the ladder is and we can pick them for you now."

"Do you think we have time?" I said, reminding Scooter of our meeting in the tree house at one o'clock.

Scooter looked at his watch. "It's only ten o'clock. We can have the apples picked in an hour and still have plenty of time."

"That'll be swell!" Mr. Henderson exclaimed. "The ladders over there, leaning on the barn. I'll get some baskets for the apples and get my trap too. I'm sure obliged to you boys."

As Scooter and I walked over to the barn I asked him, "What are you planning Scooter?"

"I'm not sure yet. I still have a few things to figure out, but the way I look at it, if this thing works out, it'll be the most fantastic plan ever devised."

Just as we came back to the tree with the ladder, Mr. Henderson came over with two baskets and the wire live trap.

"Let's set the trap first boys. I'll show you how it works."

The trap was a wire, rectangular box about twenty four inches long and eight inches square. Inside the ends of the box were two metal doors slanted down at about a forty five degree angle. A metal handle for carrying was fastened in the middle of the top of the trap.

Mr. Henderson set the trap down on the ground, reached in and raised the metal doors. Digging in his pocket he came out with a wad of wax paper. "Peanut butter." he said as he smeared it on the trigger in the center of the trap. Lifting two wires attached to the trigger, he propped up the metal doors and slid the wires under them. "There it is boys. It's simple but effective. The skunk can go in from either end and when he starts licking the peanut butter the trigger tips, knocking the wires off the metal doors causing them to fall down and trap him in there."

"Where are you going to set it?" I asked.

"Oh, I'll just put it along the wall by this hole and when he comes out he'll smell the peanut butter right away. But I don't think I'll set it today because we're going to be gone tomorrow and I wouldn't want him to be locked in there all day."

"You can set it," Scooter said. "Randy and I will come by tomorrow and check it. We can even take the skunk down the road and let him go if you catch him."

"Well, I wouldn't want to bother you boys..." Mr. Henderson said.

"It would be no bother," I insisted. "That would be fun if we caught him."

"Well, I guess if you boys don't mind doing that, I suppose we could set it today."

"We'd be glad to do it!" Scooter assured him.

"O.K." Mr. Henderson said, placing the trap along the shed wall. "But if he's in there tomorrow, you boys better be very careful when you let him out. Just raise the metal door at his head and let him walk out."

"Right," I assured him. "We'll be really careful."

"Now..." said Scooter, "Let's pick some apples."

BAITING THE TRAP

❖ ❖ ❖

Mr. Henderson helped Scooter and I get the ladder up into the apple tree. We wedged it in between some branches in the center of the tree and pushed on it to test its stability. It seemed to be fairly solid.

"Now you boys be careful and don't be reaching out any further than you have to. I don't want you getting hurt for a few apples."

"We will," Scooter said, starting up the ladder with one of the baskets. "I'll take the first turn Randy and you can take the next one."

"O.K., Scooter," I agreed. I really didn't have much choice as he was already halfway up the ladder.

Mr. Henderson squinted up at Scooter, half hidden up in the leaves of the apple tree. "How're you doing up there, son?"

"No problem! Lots of apples up here!"

"Well, if you boys can handle this, I've got some other chores I have to do."

"Go ahead Mr. Henderson," I assured him. "We can handle this."

In about ten minutes Scooter was coming down the ladder with the basket full of apples. When he came within reach he handed the basket down to me. "Your turn," he said with a grin.

"Are there lots of them?" I asked as I started up the ladder.

"Yeah, there's quite a few. It'll probably take us another hour...oh, and don't pick those on that branch hanging over the shed."

"Why not? There are some real beauties there," I called down from near the top of the ladder.

"Just because...I'll explain later."

In about half an hour Mr. Henderson returned and we had two bushel baskets full.

"Say, you boys are quite the pickers! Are there many more up there?"

"Oh, I'd say there's about another bushel up there," I said. "By the way Mr. Henderson, do you have the time?"

Mr. Henderson pulled out a pocket watch and held it out. "Just about eleven o'clock."

"We'd better hurry up Scooter," I said thinking about our one o'clock appointment with Arnold at the tree house. We still had to pedal home and come up with a plan.

"Don't worry about it boys," Mr. Henderson said. "If you have to be some place, you can come back another time and finish up. They'll stay up there for another week or so."

"Well, if you don't mind Mr. Henderson. I did tell my mom I'd be home around noon and I wouldn't want her to worry. Besides, Scooter and I can come back tomorrow when we check on the skunk trap and pick some more."

"That'd be fine. I'll leave another basket or two on the back porch in case you want to pick some more."

"And next weekend we can start on the shed," Scooter said walking over to the shed. "Let's see what this will take."

Scooter stuck his head in a window of the shed. It was more of a hole in the wall than a window, as it had no glass or frame. He looked around the inside for a minute and pulled his head back out with a secret smile on his face.

We hopped on our bikes and waved goodbye to Mr. Henderson, promising him that we'd leave the apples in his back porch and that we'd see him in a few days to make arrangements for the next weekend.

As we rode out of the yard I turned to Scooter, "You know Scooter, you were right. Mr. Henderson is a nice old man."

"He sure is, and better yet, he's given us the perfect set-up for Operation Rat Trap."

"Which reminds me…. We'd better come up with some sort of plan in a hurry."

"I think I have it pretty much figured out," Scooter said. "Give me a few more minutes until we get to the top of the hill. We'll rest there and I'll lay it out for your approval."

I might have known. Scooter had been scheming all the while we were there. This is going to interesting, I thought to myself.

At the top of the hill we pulled over and Scooter picked up his packsack from the bushes. Sitting on the bank at the side of the road, we looked down the hill at the Henderson place and Scooter explained his plan. I had to agree…It was perfect!…If it worked.

Riding back into town we went over what we were going to say in the tree house. Now hopefully Arnold would show up.

"What time is it?" I called to Scooter as we rode into town.

"Quarter to twelve...Why?"

"We can see the tree house from my room and I think we should stay up there and watch and see if Arnold shows up."

"Good idea!" Scooter said as he stood up and started pumping his bike harder.

By quarter after twelve we were up in my room with the curtains drawn almost all the way, leaving just a little opening from which we could see the tree house.

"This is just like that police stake out we saw in that movie a couple of weeks ago," Scooter said in a low voice.

"Yeah, which gives me another idea," I added.

"What's that?"

"If Arnold shows up, it would be nice to know for sure if he's going do what we want him to and when he's going to do it."

"How do you intend to find that out?" Scooter asked.

"I think this may be another case for Shelly the Spook."

"Hey!...Cool idea!" Scooter exclaimed. "We'll give her a call if Arnold shows up."

We went over our plan once more while we were waiting and were just about to rehash it again when Scooter nudged me and pointed toward the alley. Someone was sneaking along the back fence and heading toward the tree house.

Scooter looked at his watch, "Quarter to one...It looks like the Rat is taking the bait."

We watched as Arnold slowly raised his head over the back fence and looked around the back yard. He then climbed up on the fence, grabbed a branch of the big spruce tree and pulled himself up until he was just over the tree house and hidden in the thick branches.

"Let's go," I whispered to Scooter. "It's time to set the trap."

We went downstairs and out the front door. We then walked around the side of the house to make it look like we had just come in off the street. We then pretended to look around the back yard to see if the coast was clear. I'm sure Arnold was up in the tree giggling, thinking of how he had fooled us again. I couldn't believe how anyone would go so far out of their way so far to be mean. Poor Arnold! I knew in my heart that he had met his match with Scooter. He was the master schemer!

As we climbed up into the tree house Scooter turned to me, "Are you sure we're safe up here?"

"Yeah, I'm sure. Only a few kids know about this place and besides, how could anyone know when we were going to be up here?"

"I guess you're right," Scooter agreed. "I just want to make sure because this time we can't make a mistake. If anything goes wrong, the cops will be on us in a minute."

"Right!" I said a little louder than normal. "I don't want anymore trouble with the cops. That was not fun at all."

"Yeah," sneered Scooter, "And that toad face Arnold and his creep friends will never let us forget it!"

I had to put my hand over my mouth to stifle a giggle. Scooter was really laying it on thick. "So Scooter," I began, "What's the plan?"

"It's like I told you. Mr. Henderson told my mom he couldn't pick any more apples because he hurt his leg. I say we sneak out there, pick his apples for him, and show everyone that we really do good deeds."

"Sounds good," I agreed. "When and how do we do it?"

"Well, Mr. Henderson told my mom that they were leaving town for a couple of days. They're going to leave tomorrow afternoon and be back on Tuesday. I can't go tomorrow night, but we still have Monday night to do it."

"Are you sure they're not going to be home?"

"Yeah I'm sure. He said they were going to his son's house for a couple of days, and he also said they always leave a light on in the house to make it look like someone is home, so we don't have to worry."

"What'll we do with the apples when we pick them?"

"Mr. Henderson told my mom he can get five dollars a bushel down at the grocery store. I figure we can take the apples down there, sell them, and give the money to Mr. Henderson."

"How are we going to get the apples way up in the tree?"

"That's the good part. I sneaked out there this morning and scouted it out. There's a shed with a flat roof right next to the apple tree. Most of the apples are in the branches over the shed roof. I also saw a step ladder by the shed. We can use the step ladder to climb up on the shed roof, pull the ladder up after us, set it up on the flat roof and start picking apples."

"Sounds like a good plan...Are you sure you can't go tomorrow night?"

"Yeah, my grandma is coming over and I have to stay home and visit with her."

"But what if someone picks the apples in the meantime and sells them?"

"Who?" Scooter asked. "Nobody else knows about it and we're sure not going to tell anyone. I'll bet there's twenty bucks worth of apples up in that tree."

"Wow!" I exclaimed rather loudly, turning my head up toward the ceiling. I could just picture Arnold counting the money already. "Can you imagine what you could do with twenty bucks?"

"Yeah," said Scooter. "But it wouldn't be right. Those apples belong to Mr. Henderson. But you never know, maybe he'd share some of the money with us."

"You never know...You say they're leaving tomorrow night?"

"More like late afternoon. They'll be gone by the time it's dark."

"Well, I guess we'll just have to wait until Monday then. I hope this will clear our names with the cops."

"I'm sure it will," Scooter said. "At last we'll be able to show up Arnold and his Skulls."

"Yeah, they'll really be jealous of us this time!"

"Well, let's go...And remember, not a word of this to anyone!"

"My lips are sealed," I said as I started down the ladder of the tree house.

Once we were back in the house we ran up to my room and watched Arnold climb down from the Spruce tree and sneak back out along the fence.

Going back downstairs, I picked up the phone, dialed, and spoke in a low voice. "Shelly the Spook? I've got another assignment for you."

THE SETUP

❖ ❖ ❖

The phone rang about eight o'clock that night. It was Shelly the Spook reporting in. I had to hand it to her. It didn't take her long to take care of a job and from what she told me; she had done a fantastic job.

"Hello," I said picking up the phone.

"Spook," said the voice on the other end.

I decided to play along with Shelly's role as the private eye. "Check," I said. "Report on suspect."

"Suspect reported to Corner Sweet Shop. Sat in end booth with Greaseball Grogan and Bird legs Lewis. Spook sat in next booth and picked up pieces of conversation"

"What'd he say?" I interrupted.

"Patience!...Patience." Spook scolded. "Suspect is planning something for tomorrow with Grease ball and Bird legs. Something to do with apples and a shed. I couldn't hear it all but they seemed to think it was very funny."

"Did you hear a time mentioned?"

"Yes, suspect said they would meet at his house at six tomorrow evening. That's all I heard."

"You did great Spook! I owe you for this."

"There is one big favor I'd like."

"You name it Spook."

"Let me in on what's going on. If you're out to get the suspect...I'd like to be in on it."

I thought about that for a moment. Shelly had proved that she could be trusted and I didn't mind if she came in on this with us, but I had to check with Scooter first. "O.K. Spook, but I have to check with Scooter first. As far as I'm concerned it's O.K."

"Call me back after you check."

"Will do," I said hanging up the phone.

I called up Scooter and related what the Spook had told me. Scooter was as thrilled as I was. The Rat was taking the bait. I then told him what Spook had asked for.

"Gee...I don't know," Scooter replied. "What do you think? ...I mean...she is a girl."

"Well, she did help us a lot and we wouldn't know what we know now if it weren't for her. I think we should let her in. She could be a great help."

"Yeah, I guess you're right. Tell her she's in and to meet us at my house tomorrow morning at eight o'clock."

"Right! See you in the morning."

I hung up and called Shelly the Spook back. "Spook..., you are now an official member of the Zorros."

"The Zorros!" she exclaimed. "What the heck are the Zorros?"

"I'll explain everything in the morning. I can't tell you over the phone. Can you meet us at Scooter's house at eight tomorrow morning?"

"Yeah, I think so. Should I bring anything?" she asked.

"Your bike and a sack lunch. We'll see you in the morning."

"Eight o'clock...I'll be there."

The next morning I hurriedly ate breakfast, packed myself a couple of sandwiches and a jar of lemonade, and headed out for Scooter's. Eagle One was sitting on his front steps waiting for me when I arrived. A big hammer and a bow saw were lying at the foot of the steps.

"What's with the tools?" I asked.

"You'll see...Where's the Spook?"

"I told her to meet us at eight," I said looking up the street. "Here she comes now."

Shelly rode up dressed in blue jeans and a sweatshirt, her light brown hair tied back in a pony tail. She greeted us with a big grin. "Hi guys! What's up?"

"C'mon over, Spook," I called. "We'll fill you in on the deal."

Shelly parked her bike and came and sat on the steps with us.

"First of all," I began. "You have to swear never to breathe a word of what you are about to hear. It could mean big trouble for all of us."

"I swear," said Shelly "that I won't say a word to anyone, even if they put a fishhook through my tongue and pull me up a flagpole."

"Yuk!" I said. "Where'd you ever hear that one?"

"I made it up...pretty neat huh?"

"Yeah," said Scooter. "O.K...Here's the deal."

Scooter began with the beginning of how we came to form the Zorros club and our first target. I jumped in and added details and carried the story further. Shelly's eyes grew wider and wider as we went along. We told of how our target was ruined at Mrs. Bronson's house and of how we suspected that Arnold and the Skulls were the culprits. We explained how we were framed with my lunch ticket and Scooter's math paper and the trouble we were into with the cops. We then mapped out our plan for Operation Rat Bait and Operation Rat Trap. Scooter told of our code names and of the secret ways in which we communicated.

"Now that you're in it," I said. "You'll have to have a code name too."

"I'd like to keep on being the Spook," Shelly said in a low voice. "I kind of like that name."

"Yeah," said Scooter. "That's a neat name. So Spook, what do you think of everything we told you?"

"All I can say is...Wow! I never realized that you guys were in as much trouble as you are. But don't worry. If I know you guys, you'll come out O.K. and Arnold and the Skulls will pay."

"If everything goes right." Scooter replied. "I'll fill you and Randy in on the rest of the plan when we get to the target. Let's get going."

As we came to the top of the hill overlooking the Henderson place, we stopped to rest. Scooter pointed down at the quiet little farm and commented. "That flat roofed shed is the key to the whole operation. Let's sit on the bank over here and I'll lay out the rest of my plan for your approval. Maybe you guys can think of a wrinkle or two that we can add."

Spook and I slapped our legs and laughed when Scooter finished telling of his plan. It was unreal how he came up with such neat plans, right down to each detail. This was going to be fun to set up and watch!

"Let's do it!" Scooter said, picking up his bike and pointing down the hill.

A few minutes later we cruised down the Henderson driveway. Just as Mr. Henderson said, nobody was home and we had the whole place to ourselves for the day and, with his permission.

"Let's finish picking the apples first and then do our thing," I suggested.

"Good idea," Scooter said. "I'll get the baskets."

There were not a lot of apples left, but we did manage to pick two more small baskets, leaving the two branches that hung over the shed roof. Looking at those two branches, I saw that they were just high enough over the roof to have to use a stepladder to pick.

We put the apples in Mr. Henderson's back porch and covered the baskets with an old rug. We weren't taking any chances that this plan might backfire.

"What's next?" Spook asked as we came out of the porch.

"Well," Scooter said. "You two can take the big ladder down out of the tree and I'll get the old stepladder I saw by the shed."

"Scooter!" I exclaimed. "We forgot to check the trap!"

Scooter's mouth dropped open for a moment before we took off running toward the shed. I came to a screeching halt and raised my hand before we turned the corner of the shed.

"Easy...easy," I warned. "We'd better be careful before we go charging in. This may be like handling a live bomb."

Three heads peeked slowly around the corner of the shed.

There along the shed wall lay the live trap, both trap doors down and black and white hair poking out through the wire sides.

"Yes!" Scooter whispered as he clapped us on the back.

We tip-toed up to the trap. Mr. Henderson was right. The big Skunk was jammed so tightly into the trap that he couldn't raise his tail. Shelly wasn't too sure if that was really true and hung back a little.

"C'mon Spook," Scooter said hunching down by the trap. "He can't spray you if he can't pull the trigger."

Shelly walked slowly over to the trap and knelt down by Scooter. She hesitated a moment and then slowly reached out and touched the fur sticking out through the wires. "I never thought that I would ever touch a wild Skunk." She said, then added. "He's kind of cute, isn't he?"

I had to admit that he was kind of cute, but wasn't sure I wanted to pet him. "Now what?" I asked.

Scooter picked up the trap by the handle. "For now, let's just put him off to the side where he won't get excited. When we're ready we'll put him into action."

I helped him carry the trap over into the shade of a small bush about fifty feet away. Shelly had overcome any fear of the Skunk by now and was kneeling down, peering into the trap.

"I wonder if a person could tame a Skunk?" she asked.

"Yeah," I commented. "Some people catch Skunks when they're real little, remove their scent glands, and keep them for pets."

"Wow! That would be neat to have a skunk for a pet!"

"Yeah it would," I agreed. "C'mon, let him rest and calm down, we have other work to do."

Shelly and I walked back to the shed while Scooter went to get his packsack and tools. Shelly opened the door of the shed and peered in.

"Whew!" She said, making a twisted face. "That smell makes your eyes water! What the heck was in there?"

"Pig and chicken manure," I said with a smile. "I'd say a couple of year's worth by the looks of the depth of it."

"Yuk! It must be eight inches deep."

"At least." I laughed.

Scooter returned with the tools and the packsack. He dug around in the sack and brought forth a pair of high rubber boots and a flashlight.

"You're going in there?" Shelly asked.

"Have to," Scooter said, tying a big handkerchief around his face, cowboy style. "When the going gets tough, the tough get going."

Scooter went in first with just the flashlight to check it out. A couple of minutes later he came out pulling down the handkerchief with a wide grin.

"Perfect!" he exclaimed. "C'mon, I'll show you."

"No thanks Scooter," I replied. "We believe you. Just tell us what you saw."

"You don't have to go in. Just stand by the door and I'll show you."

Scooter held the door back and shined the light in as we stood and peered into the dim light of the shed.

"See that center post?" he said, pointing the light. "That's the main support of the roof. The rafters are all pretty well rotted and if the post is gone, there's very little holding the roof up."

"So you're going to take out the post." I commented.

"Right! With a little weight on the roof, it should come tumbling down"

"With Arnold and Bird legs and Grease ball," Shelly giggled.

"You got the picture!" Scooter laughed.

THE TRAP

❖ ❖ ❖

Scooter put the handkerchief back over his face and went to work. Once inside the shed he discovered that he didn't need the saw as the post was rotted off at the bottom. He began pounding on the post near the bottom and the whole shed shook with the vibrations.

"Hold it!" Shelly shouted in the doorway. "It looks to me as if the roof is going to fall in if you take the post out. I don't think that's going to work."

I had to agree with her. I didn't think the shed was as sturdy as we had originally thought. "She's right Scooter. I think the whole works will come down if you take the post out."

Scooter stuck his head back out the door and pulled down the handkerchief. "Great...and I'll be in there when it does. Do you guys have any better ideas?"

The three of us stood there and studied the problem for a few moments. This was a no win situation. If we took the post out, the shed roof would fall in, ruining our trap. If we didn't take the post out, it wouldn't fall in, ruining our trap. There had to be another way, but I couldn't think of one.

Shelly earned her right to be a Zorro when she came up with her idea.

"This reminds me of a trap I saw in a book about Indians," she began. "They would have a big log or weight of some kind propped up by a post like this. Then they would have some kind of bait tied to a rope and to the post and when the animal grabbed the bait, it would knock the post loose and the big log would fall on it."

Scooter studied the shed and scratched his head. "Hmm... I think that would work, but we may have to change a few things."

I walked around the shed, thinking, looking, and coming up with a few ideas of my own. I looked from the shed to the yard and back to the shed. Suddenly the idea hit me like a bolt of lightning.

"Hey guys! Come here!" I shouted. "Shelly is right! This trap is just like one of those Indian traps, and we're going to be the Indians."

"What do you mean?" Scooter asked.

I pointed over at a large dog house about forty feet away. "If we can find a long enough rope, we can tie it to the bottom of the post and run it under the wall and over to that dog house."

"And then what?" Scooter laughed. "Get a big dog and teach him to pull on the rope when they're up on the roof?"

"Very funny Scooter. I thought you'd be clever enough to be ahead of me on this one. Can't you see? We'll hide in the doghouse tonight and when they get up on the roof... pull!"

Scooter looked at Shelly and raised his eyebrows. "Not bad...not bad at all."

Shelly snapped her fingers, "And best of all, we'll be right here to see all the action and nobody will see us."

"Perfect!" I exclaimed. "Let's find some rope. Mr. Henderson should have some around here someplace."

The garage was open and we went in and searched every nook and cranny. We found a few pieces of short rope and a broken chain or two, but nothing that would fit our needs.

"Let's try the barn." Scooter suggested.

As we entered the dimly lit barn we could see that it hadn't been used for years. All we could see were a few empty cow stalls and some old bales of hay. There wasn't a rope to be found.

"How about up in the hay mow?" Shelly suggested, pointing at a ladder on the wall that led to a square hole in the ceiling.

"Good idea! I said as I ran over to the ladder. In single file we slowly climbed up the crude ladder that was nailed to the wall and entered a huge empty cavern on the second floor of the barn.

"Holy mackerel!" Scooter exclaimed. "We could set up a basketball court up here!"

"Yeah, it's huge, but I don't see any rope."

"Now what?" Shelly asked as we climbed back down the ladder.

"I don't know. You'd think he'd have some rope around here somewhere. Let's try out behind the barn." I said pointing to the back door.

Near the back door on the left side we noticed a small room with a tall wooden door. We pulled back the door and found a light string hanging from the ceiling. Scooter pulled the string, flooding the tiny area with light. Hanging from the walls were old musty smelling horse collars, reins, halters, and all the other old kinds of horse equipment a farmer would need. Turning around we spied on the wall by the door what appeared to be miles of rope, all neatly coiled and hanging on big nails pounded into the wall.

"Bingo!" I shouted.

We took down a big coil of half inch rope and stretched it out in the long barn. Shelly and I stood at one end of the barn while Scooter uncoiled it. He reached the front door of the barn and kept on going. Stopping about twenty feet out, he called back to us.

"This will be more than enough! Let's get to work!"

We hauled the rope over to the shed and dropped it on the ground.

"You go inside, Scooter, and I'll pass the rope through this hole in the bottom board." I suggested.

"Wait a minute," Shelly said, holding the end of the rope. "Why don't we make sure the post is loose first? I don't want to be sitting in that doghouse pulling on a post that won't come loose."

"Good idea," Scooter said, pulling the handkerchief back up over his mouth and nose.

Shelly and I stood outside while Scooter went to work with the big hammer. We could hear the dull thuds as he pounded at the bottom of the post. We could also hear the slurp of his boots as he walked around in the gooey manure. We were glad that it was him in there and not us.

In about ten minutes Scooter stepped out the door and pulled down his face mask and proclaimed, "The bottoms loose."

"What about the top?" I asked.

"That's next. I had to take a break. A guy can only stand it in there so long."

In a few minutes, Scooter went back in and started working on the top of the post. With a few well placed blows from the hammer and a little pushing on Scooter's part, the post came loose and tipped to the side. The roof began to sag and Scooter quickly pushed the post back into place.

He stuck his head out the door and called, "Put the rope through and I'll tie it up."

I ran around the shed and picked up the rope, pushing the end through the hole in the bottom board. Shelly stayed by the door and watched as Scooter took the rope, wrapped it around the bottom of the post a couple of times and then tied a sturdy knot.

"Stomp it down into the gook," Shelly suggested. "In case they look in the door."

Scooter didn't answer. I don't think he was wild about taking orders from a girl, but he didn't argue and walked the line of the rope until it disappeared down in the gooey mess on the floor.

I picked up the other end of the rope and walked over to the dog house. It reached the dog house door with about eight feet to spare. I tucked the other end into the dog house and ran back to the shed just as Scooter was coming out the door.

He brushed off his hands and grinned, "All set."

"What about the skunk?" I asked.

Scooter grinned again. "There's a little dry spot in the corner with a small pen about three feet square. It must have been a place for a setting hen or something, but it'll be perfect for our black and white friend. He won't be able to get out of it and yet it's open enough to give him room to shoot. We can put some of that old hay from the barn in there and he'll be nice and dry."

"Shall we go and get him?" Shelly asked.

"No, I don't think so; let's wait until just before we leave. The less time he's in there the better he'll be."

"I'll leave half of my sandwich in there for him." I volunteered.

"Good idea," Scooter said. "Which reminds me, I'm hungry?"

"You must have a cast iron stomach," Shelly said sticking out her tongue and twisting her face. "How can you think about food after slopping around in there?"

"Easy!" Scooter laughed. "I worked up an appetite working in there."

We sat under the apple tree and munched on our sandwiches and drank our lemonade. It was about eleven thirty and we were just about done. We felt that we had accomplished a lot in a couple of hours.

"What's next?" Shelly said, crumpling up her lunch sack.

"I don't know," Scooter said. "The skunk is the only thing left that I can think of. How about you guys?"

"Well, I've been thinking," I said. "I think we should see if we're all going to fit in the dog house and then I think we should take some of that old hay from the barn and scatter it over the rope. We wouldn't want them to find the rope with us at the other end of it."

"Good idea," Shelly replied. "And I was wondering if we shouldn't take Scooter's saw and saw part way through the rafters...Just to make sure the trap will work."

"Hey!" exclaimed Scooter. "That is a good idea! I knew there was a good reason why we brought you into the Zorros, Spook."

"And we'd better hurry," I insisted. "We can't afford to be seen around here in case Arnold and the Skulls decide to scout the place out."

"Right!" Scooter and Shelly said together.

Scooter put on his mask and boots again and entered the shed with the saw. Peeking through the side window, Shelly and I watched as he sawed part way into the old rotten rafters. In ten minutes he emerged from the smelly shed, pulled down his face mask and gave us the thumbs up signal with a big grin.

In a short time we had carried two bales of the old hay from the barn. We broke open one bale and scattered the hay along the rope from the dog house to the shed. We then scattered some in other places around the tree to make it look natural. Scooter then broke open the second bale, pulled up his face mask, and picked up a big armload.

He stepped through the door with his skunk bedding and we could hear him rustling around in the darkness of the shed. In a minute or so he stepped back out with a big grin.

"Let's go get Stinky and show him his new home."

"How're you going to get him out of the trap?" Shelly asked.

Scooter thought about that a moment. "I think I'll just set the cage down in the little pen and very carefully lift up the trap doors. I'll leave the trap right there. He can walk out when he wants to and we can pick up the trap next weekend when we clean up the wreckage."

"Wreckage?" I asked. "You don't think those guys will get hurt do you?"

"I...don't think so." Scooter answered.

"Maybe we should throw a few buckets of water in there to make it softer." I suggested.

"And sloppier!" Shelly exclaimed. "What a super idea!"

A short time later we found several buckets in the garage, filled them from an outside faucet on the house and each made two trips to the shed. Standing in the doorway we threw in the water and then watched as Scooter went back in and stomped around mixing it into a gooey mess. The only thing left now was to deposit the Skunk and wait for tonight.

STINKY

❖ ❖ ❖

Scooter and I went and picked up the skunk trap very carefully and brought it back to the shed. The skunk didn't seem to mind being in the trap as he just looked at us and blinked a few times. We set the trap down by the door as Scooter pulled up his face mask and picked up his flashlight.

Shelly and I watched from the doorway as Scooter entered the shed with the skunk and the trap. Slowly he made his way over to the dry corner and carefully set it down in the little pen in the corner. He then reached in his pocket and took out the half sandwich I had given him. He placed it along the far side of the wire pen so the skunk would have to come out of the trap to reach it.

Turning to us he whispered, "Here goes nothing."

Slowly he reached in and raised the two metal doors of the trap. Flipping a little catch on the side of the trap, he locked the doors in place. The skunk didn't move as Scooter stood up and quietly moved back to the door.

"Let's go watch through the window," Scooter whispered as he pulled down his face mask.

We quietly closed the door and softly walked around the shed to the side window. We could just barely squeeze our three heads in the window, but we managed. The skunk pen was on the opposite side so we had a good view of the trap. For a minute or so the skunk just sat there and didn't move. He then moved his front feet and stuck his head out of the trap, smelling the sandwich that Scooter had left in the hay in front of the trap. In another minute he had squeezed himself out of the trap and began munching on the sandwich. We looked at each other, nodding our heads and smiling. It looked like Stinky was going to be comfortable until tonight.

"C'mon," I said as we left the shed. "Let's see if we can fit in the dog house and then get out of here."

Scooter took off running toward the dog house. "Last one in is a skunks brother!"

I didn't mind being the skunk's brother as Scooter banged his head on the door trying to get in. Shelly pushed him in before he could say anything and I kneeled and looked in before entering. Scooter sat in one corner holding his head while Shelly sat next to him in the other corner trying not to laugh. I crawled in and looked around. It was crowded, but we did fit. It was an awfully big dog house.

"What do you think guys?" I asked.

"It's crowded," Scooter said. "But it'll work. I just hope they don't spot us in here."

"We can pull some of that hay in the doorway and besides, it'll be almost dark by six thirty," I replied. "We should be back here and in the dog house by six."

"Sounds good, let's go." Scooter said.

We jumped on our bikes and headed back to town, talking back and forth of all the possibilities that might happen. We stopped at the top of the first hill and looked back down at the Henderson place. It looked all quiet. Shelly was riding in front and she raised her hand to stop when we came to the top of Taylor's Hill. She quickly turned her bike around and waved us back as she came toward us.

"The skulls are coming!" She exclaimed. "Take the bikes and hide in the brush!"

We could see that she was serious, so we didn't argue. We jumped off of our bikes and followed Shelly off the road and into the bushes. After about thirty feet she dropped her bike and lay down alongside it. We copied her.

I finally recovered enough to ask, "Who's coming, Shell?"

"Arnold, Bird legs, and Grease ball," She panted. "They're riding bikes up the hill."

"Did they see you?" Scooter asked.

"No...Quiet now!" Shelly whispered, pointing toward the road.

We watched through the bushes as the three Skulls rode into view. For a moment I thought they were going to stop and rest, but they just slowed down and cruised right by us.

Wow, that was close!" Scooter said, wiping his forehead.

"I'll bet they're going to case out the place," I said.

"For sure," Shelly added. "I just hope they don't go snooping around the place."

"No way," I assured her. "Arnold thinks Mr. Henderson is still home and I don't think he's going to take a chance after Mr. Henderson threatened to cut his hands off with a hacksaw."

We all laughed at that as we pictured Arnold running through the bushes with Mr. Henderson shouting threats at him. Hopefully tonight we'd all get even.

Riding back into town we decided to go up in my tree house and make some final plans. There were still some details to be worked out. We wanted to find a way to let Inspector 4 in on this without him knowing it was us.

"Maybe we should call him and just tell him what we're up to." Scooter suggested.

"Nahh...," I disagreed. "He'll probably think its too dangerous or something and call a halt to it. There's got to be a better way."

"How about an anonymous tip?" Shelly suggested.

"A what?" We both said.

Shelly looked at us in disgust. "You know, a phone call to the police when you don't tell them who is calling. We can just tell them when and where to be."

"That might work." I agreed. "We can try it."

"O.K." said Scooter, "But we won't call until just before we leave. We don't want them coming too early."

"What time shall we leave?" Shelly asked.

"I'd say about...five thirty. That would put us out there about a half hour before the Skulls and time enough to check on Stinky and anything else that might come up."

Before we left we all agreed on the cover story we were going to tell our moms. An evening ball game at the playground was a good enough story to place us all in the same place at the same time.

I was just about to start down the ladder of the tree house when a thought suddenly came into my head. "The ladder! Scooter! What about the step ladder to get up on the shed roof? We forgot about it!"

Scooter looked at me with a little smile, "You forgot about it...I didn't. Don't worry, it's there. I put it alongside the shed while you guys were scattering the hay around."

Whew! What a relief! I thought for a moment that our plans would go down the drain because of one little detail.

We agreed to meet back here at the tree house at five fifteen and went our separate ways. I spent the afternoon helping mom around the house with some chores, trying to keep busy to pass the time. At long last the clock finally showed five o'clock and a few minutes later Shelly and Scooter showed up together. I guess they couldn't wait any longer either. We decided to head out a little early as there was no point in waiting around any longer.

The sun was dipping down toward the trees as we climbed on our bikes and headed out. It would be dark in another hour, just about right for everything to fall into place. Scooter rode in front with his packsack on his back, bulging with his flashlight and some other goodies he had tucked in there in the last minute. The butterflies in my stomach began to flutter as we made our way up Taylor's Hill. **Operation Rat Trap** was about to begin.

NOW WHAT?

❖ ❖ ❖

The Henderson yard was in long shadows as we rode up the driveway and hid our bikes in the barn. We took another look at our furry friend in the shed and he was curled up in the hay taking a long nap. It looked as if everything was in order and ready for the arrival of Arnold and the Skulls.

"C'mon guys," I suggested. "Let's get in the dog house before they get here. It'll be dark in another twenty minutes."

"Yeah," Scooter agreed. "We don't want to get caught out in the open and spoil everything after all the work we went through. Besides, we can pull some hay over the door and use my flashlight for light inside."

Shelly crawled in first and sat crosswise across the back wall. Scooter and I crawled in backward with our heads toward the door and curled our legs up to squeeze our bodies in all the way. We then pulled some loose hay up around the door to hide any movement. We were all set. All we had to do now was wait for the action to start.

Scooter flicked on his flashlight and looked at his watch. "Ten after six," he commented. "If they met at Arnold's at six, they should be about half way here...I'd say about another fifteen minutes."

We sat in silence for about a minute as time dragged on. Shelly and I squirmed around in the darkness to get a better view. I found a small crack by the door to watch through, while Scooter and Shelly shared the door.

The big moment had finally arrived. I felt excited about what was about to happen and yet something was nagging at the back of my mind. It seemed that we had forgotten something and I couldn't remember what. In my mind I began going over the steps of **Operation Rat Trap**, trying to pin point what was bothering me. All of a sudden it hit me like a bolt of lightning!

"Scooter!" I cried. "We forgot to call Inspector 4!"

Scooter looked at me with a look of horror on his face. Somehow in the urgency of getting ready, we all had forgotten the key element of **Operation Rat Trap**. Now what?

"Do the Henderson's have a phone?" Shelly quickly asked.

"Yeah," I answered, "But the house is locked and I don't know if we have enough time anyway."

"C'mon," Scooter said, crawling out of the dog house. "I know where the key is and we've got to try!"

"What time is it?" I asked.

"Six twenty," Scooter said over his shoulder as we raced toward the house.

We jumped up on the back porch and Scooter lifted up a flower pot on the window sill revealing the house key.

"It's a good thing Mr. Henderson happened to mention where he hid the key or for sure we'd be dead ducks!"

"And how!" I agreed. "Hurry up with the key...we have only a few minutes!"

Scooter inserted the key and turned the lock. He gave us a wink and a half smile as the knob turned and the door opened. Now came the scary part. I didn't like the idea of going into someone's house like this and if we ever got caught, we'd really be in trouble.

"Use the flashlight!" Shelly whispered as we entered the kitchen.

Scooter slowly shined the light around the old fashioned kitchen. There on the wall by the doorway to the living room was the phone.

"I wonder where they keep the phone book." I asked.

Scooter shined the light around. "I don't know...but we'd better find it in a hurry."

Shelly reached over our shoulders and pointed at the wall. "Here's the police and fire number taped to the wall by the phone."

"Way to go, Shelly!" I said, patting her on the back. I was really proud of her and what she had done for us these last few days.

"Who's going to make the phone call to Inspector 4?" Scooter asked.

"You call," I said, afraid that I would panic and forget what to say.

"All right," Scooter said picking up the phone and dialing.

Shelly and I listened intently, waiting to hear what Scooter was going to say.

"Hello," Scooter said, "I'd like to speak to Inspector 4 please."

Scooter held the phone out far enough so Shelly and I could hear and the voice on the other end wasn't very pleasant.

"Who?" growled the voice.

"Inspector 4," Scooter said more slowly.

"Is this some kind of a joke?" The voice said.

"No sir, we were told to call this number by Inspector 4. He said everyone at the police station would know who he was."

"Just a minute..." We heard the man shout to someone else, asking if they knew anything about an Inspector 4. We next heard a lot of laughing from several people and also from the voice on the other end.

"Is there a problem?" Scooter asked.

"No, son,"... more giggles. "Uhh...Inspector 4 is busy on assignment right now. Can I take a message?"

"Yes, listen carefully. It's important that you reach Inspector 4 in the next hour or so. Tell him that the Zorro's have set a trap and the real vandals are about to strike. Tell him he should come up Mill Pond Road at about seven o'clock and park on the back side of Taylor's Hill, where he can see the Henderson farm. Tell him to watch for three flashes from a flashlight. That will be his signal to come down at full speed with lights flashing and siren wailing."

"Is that all?" said the voice.

"Ummm...no," said Scooter. "Tell him also to have another policeman come along in an unmarked pickup truck."

Shelly and I looked at each other with a questioning look. What in the world was Scooter up to now?

"O.K." said the voice. "Let me read this back to you."

He read the message back to Scooter and it was the same.

"That's right, sir, and please see that he gets it as soon as possible. If he isn't there by seven, he'll miss the arrest of his life."

"We'll do our best to be there." said the voice. "Thanks for the tip."

"You're welcome," Scooter said placing the phone down and grinning at us.

"A pickup truck?" I asked.

"You'll see," Scooter smiled. "Just wait."

Shelly called from the kitchen window where she had been watching the road. "Let's get out of here! They're coming down the hill!"

We ran out the back door, quickly relocked the house, put the key back under the flower pot, jumped off the porch and sneaked around the side of the house to see how close they were.

Just in time! Arnold and the skulls were at the bottom of the hill and just about to pass by the Henderson house.

Scooter turned to us, "When they pass between the house and us, we'll make a run for the dog house."

Shelly and I didn't argue. There wasn't time. We nodded our heads in agreement and prepared to dash across the yard.

"Now!" Scooter whispered, and we took off for the dog house. It only took us about five seconds to cross the yard and another five seconds to dive into the doghouse.

Scrambling around in the crowded, dark space, we managed to twist ourselves around so we all could see. Scooter and Shelly shared the door, while I found a wide crack in the wall alongside of them. Although it was almost dark we could still make out Arnold and the Skulls riding by the driveway.

They rode by a little ways and then stopped and hid their bikes in the weeds alongside the road. Walking back, they stood on the road and checked out the Henderson place for a full minute before entering.

Arnold, Grease ball, and Bird legs tiptoed in a half crouch along the driveway, carrying a couple of bushel baskets. Twice they stopped and studied the house to see if anyone was home. Seeing the coast was clear, they went directly to the shed. They were confident that nobody was home and they were speaking loud enough for us to hear from the dog house.

"Here's the ladder," Arnold said, picking up the stepladder and placing it against the wall. "You guys know what to do."

Arnold climbed up the ladder first. It didn't quite reach the top of the wall, so he had to lift his leg up on the roof and roll himself over and up. The shed squeaked and groaned a little as he stood up.

"Watch it!" he called down. "This thing isn't too sturdy"

Scooter turned to us with a loud whisper. "He doesn't think it's sturdy now...He ain't seen nothing yet!"

Shelly and I covered our mouths to stifle a nervous giggle. This was more exciting than I had ever dreamed it would be.

Arnold now leaned down and gave a helping hand to Grease ball and Bird legs as they crawled up on the roof. He then leaned over the edge and grasped the ladder by the top step and pulled it up on the roof. Grease ball helped him pull the legs out and set it up under the overhanging apple tree limbs.

Arnold picked up one of the bushel baskets that the other boys had handed up and placed his foot on the first rung of the stepladder.

"One of you guys hold the ladder steady for me and the other stand back and keep watch. I don't think all of us should be putting our weight in one place."

Grease ball grabbed the stepladder and steadied it while Bird legs stepped back a few feet. Arnold slowly climbed up the stepladder until his head and shoulders disappeared in the leaves of the apple tree. Reaching down, he grabbed the basket Grease ball was handing up and placed it on the top step of the ladder.

"Any apples up there?" Grease ball called to him.

"Loads of them," Arnold said laughing. "Randy and Scooter are in for a big surprise tomorrow."

"Not as big as the one you're in for tonight, Arnold," I mumbled to myself.

A series of steady thuds could be heard from up on the stepladder as Arnold dropped the apples into the basket. I was hoping he wouldn't get them all.

"Maybe we should pull the rope before he cleans out the tree," I whispered.

Scooter looked at his watch. "No, it's only five to seven. We have to wait until at least seven to make sure Inspector 4 gets here."

Arnold had filled one of the small bushel baskets and handed it down to Grease ball. He then began filling the second basket and from the sound of the thuds it wouldn't take long to fill the second one.

"What time?" I whispered.

"Seven," Scooter answered. "Let's wait a few more minutes."

"If he gets that second basket filled, it'll be too late." I argued.

"Yeah, I guess you're right..." Scooter agreed. "O.K. lets do it!"

We pulled in the slack from the rope and tightened it up. We leaned back in the dog house, braced our feet against the front wall and pulled.

We couldn't budge it! Evidently the weight of the three boys on the roof was pushing down on the post.

"Give it a little slack and then jerk hard," Scooter ordered. "Ready?...one...two...three!"

We all tumbled hard against the back wall as the post gave way. Quickly we scrambled around to watch.

Our mouths dropped open as we saw all three boys still up on the roof.

"Whoa!" Arnold called down. "What the heck happened?"

"I don't know," Grease ball called back. "Something gave way and the roof sagged a little, but we're O.K."

"Well, let's finish up and get out of here." Arnold said.

I couldn't believe it and neither could Scooter or Spook. After all of our work and planning, it wasn't working! I closed my eyes for a second, fighting back panic. We had to act and act fast!

CREATURES FROM THE BLACK LAGOON

❖ ❖ ❖

I squeezed my eyes shut, concentrating on what to do. If Arnold and the skulls got away after we had called the police, they would for sure think we were guilty and just be trying to throw them off the track. I felt our only chance was to try to have them catch Arnold and the Skulls on the roof, or at least in the Henderson yard.

I shoved Scooter and Shelly over as I grabbed the flashlight and crawled out the door.

"What're you doing?" Scooter said in a loud whisper.

"Shhh!" I said turning to him. I didn't have time to explain as I crawled behind the doghouse and pointed the flashlight up the road toward the top of Taylor's hill. I clicked the on switch three times and waited.

Bird legs cried out from the shed roof. "What was that light?

"What light?" Arnold called from up in the apple tree.

"I thought I saw a light out in the yard."

"I didn't see any light."

"I'm sure there was a light."

"Ahhh...you're seeing things. Besides, we'll be done in a few minutes and we can get out of here."

I sat behind the doghouse, not daring to crawl around and back in again. Where were the police? In desperation I again pointed the flashlight up toward the hill and flashed three times.

"There it is again!" called Bird legs. "Let's get out of here!"

"Where?"

"Over there...in the yard!"

Just then, the long wail of a siren pierced the still night air. I turned and looked up at Taylor's hill as headlights came on and then red and blue flashing lights sprayed across the woods and fields as the car came down toward us. A second pair of headlights followed the first car down the hill in a cloud of dust.

I poked my head up over the dog house as Grease ball shouted, "Cops! Let's get out of here!"

With the glow from the approaching headlights, we could see the three shadowy figures up on the pig pen roof. Arnold was still up on the top of the stepladder, frozen with fear for a moment. As the police car reached the bottom of the hill Arnold overcame his panic and made his move.

Leaning over on the already rickety ladder he called to Grease ball. "Here...grab this bushel basket!"

That was their final mistake! Grease ball let go of the ladder to grab the bushel basket and Arnold, off balance from leaning over, felt the ladder pushing out from under him. To save himself from falling face first, he made a desperate leap out from the ladder and came down feet first alongside Grease ball. With the support post gone, the sawed through rafters did their work! With a loud, tearing, crash, the roof folded in the middle and broke in half, sending the Skulls sliding rapidly down into the gooey pig manure.

Now of course, our friend Stinky didn't take too kindly to strangers dropping in on him like that and he let them know about it and quickly. It was also evident from the screams and yells that the Skulls thought about as much of Stinky as they did the pig manure. All in all it was a most satisfying and hilarious scene.

Scooter and Shelly had crawled out and joined me behind the doghouse as the roof caved in. Now we all three leaned over the dog house with just our heads peeking over the roofline.

We could hold our silence no longer. We roared with laughter and slapped each other on the backs as we listened to the Skulls yelling and cursing, mixed with the sound of breaking boards and gooshy pig manure as they repeatedly fell down in their desperation to get out.

Stinky's odor hit us as the police headlights turned into the yard. We ducked down behind the dog house and covered our noses and mouths from the smell. I couldn't imagine what it must have been like inside the pig shed, as I had all I could do to stand the smell over behind the dog house.

We peeked our heads back up over the roof as the siren died down and the police jumped out of their car. Two super bright spotlights lit up the pig shed as the police shouted, "Come out with your hands up!"

The first one out was Stinky and he didn't stop for anyone...police or no police. They in turn did not try to stop him as the spotlights followed him, running as fast as his little legs could carry him toward the woods and safety.

The spotlights flashed back to the shed as a croaking voice from within called out, "Don't shoot! We're coming out."

I couldn't begin to tell you who crawled out first, as they all looked the same. They reminded me of the monster we had seen in a horror movie a couple of weeks ago, _The Creature from the Black Lagoon_. They were totally covered in dripping, slimy pig manure, from head to foot and reeked from Stinky's gift of perfume. Even the police didn't want to get close to them.

"You boys just stay where you are until we can figure out what to do with you." called one policeman.

Arnold, Grease ball, and Bird legs started crying as they stood there in the spotlight, cold, humiliated, scared, and reeking to high heaven. You may not believe this, but for a moment I actually felt sorry for them.

"C'mon," Scooter whispered, "I've got an idea."

"What's that?" I asked.

"Let's sneak over there and talk to Inspector 4."

"I don't think that's such a good idea."

"Leave it to me...We can't let them standing there all night."

"Oh...all right."

"You boys go ahead. I'll stay here." Shelly said. "I don't want the police to know I've been involved. My parents would ground me for two years if they found out I was here."

"I understand." I said. "Wait here…we won't be long."

We half crawled and sneaked around and behind the police car. It was hard to tell who was who in the dark, but after a few moments we were able to make out Inspector 4 standing alongside the police car.

Scooter poked his head around the back of the car and whispered, "Pssst!…Inspector 4!"

Inspector 4 turned and walked to the back of the police car. "Well, hello boys," he said with a big smile. " I thought maybe that was you out there in the light."

"No," Scooter whispered, "And could you please keep it down. We don't want anyone to know we're here."

"Alright," he whispered back. "Did you boys do this?"

Not knowing for sure what his reaction would be, I decided to lie. "No sir, we just happened to be in the neighborhood and we heard the siren, so we came over to see what was happening."

"Oh, I see…" Inspector 4 said. I could tell by the little smile on his face that he didn't really believe us.

"May I offer a suggestion?" Scooter asked.

"Yeah…I could use some help with this one."

Scooter pointed over toward the barn. "There's an old stock tank over by the barn that they used to use for watering cows. It's about half full of water. Why don't you have those guys take their clothes off and wash up in that tank. Then you can wrap them up in some blankets or something and have them ride back to town in the back of your pickup."

Inspector 4 put his hand up to his face and rubbed his chin for a few moments. "Hmmm…That might work. I for sure don't want them riding in the squad car in the condition that they're in."

I grinned to myself as I realized that Scooter had this planned all along. Now I knew why he told the police to bring a pickup truck.

Inspector 4 turned and called to another policeman, "Bill, do you have any blankets in the squad car?"

"Yeah, there are three or four in the trunk."

Inspector 4 pointed toward the barn, "Shine the spotlight over there. There's an old stock tank there that these boys can wash up in. Then we'll wrap them in the blankets and they can ride in the back of the pickup."

"Good idea!" came the answering voice. "C'mon boys, lets go over by the barn."

Inspector 4 turned to us again. "Can I give you kids a lift back to town?"

"No thanks sir," I said. "We've got our bikes here and it's a nice night for a ride."

"Oh, and sir?" Scooter jumped in. "Remember, mums the word."

"My lips are sealed," Inspector 4 said as he turned and walked off to help with the cleanup.

We disappeared around the police car and made our way back to the dog house. Shelly was still waiting for us and anxious to hear what happened. "Well, what did he say? Is he going to arrest them? Are they going to jail?" She questioned.

"I don't know about arresting them or taking them to jail, but they're going to do something that I don't think you should watch." Scooter giggled.

Shelly looked at the two of us smirking. She tilted her head, squinted, and asked, "What's so funny?"

"You'll see." I said. "But you'll have to turn your head when we tell you."

Shelly mumbled something under her breath about boys, but agreed that she'd go along with us. We circled back around the house in the dark and sneaked up to the backdoor of the barn. From here we entered the dark cavern of cow stalls and moldy hay and crept up to the window nearest to the stock tank.

We had front row seats as the tank was only a few yards from the window. Peeking our heads up, we watched as Arnold, Grease ball, and Bird legs slowly peeled off their manure covered clothes. When they got down to their underwear, I placed my hand on Shelly's head and slowly pushed her down from the window. She slid down and sat with her back to the wall, not wanting to see what was coming next. One policeman picked up the clothes with a stick and pushed them down into a big plastic garbage bag, while the other found an old pail and began pouring cold water from the tank over the shivering naked boys.

All three boys sniffled and blubbered while the cold water was poured over them. I'm sure it was a combination of humiliation, embarrassment, and the shock of the cold water as they stood naked in the spotlight. Again, I felt a pang of sympathy for them..., but only for a moment, as I reminded myself that they were only getting what they had brought upon themselves.

The police then handed each of them a blanket and ordered them into the back of the pickup. With the squad car in the lead, they turned and drove out of the yard and up the road to Taylor's Hill.

We were just getting our bikes from behind the barn when once again the yard was lit up by headlights. Cautiously we peeked around the barn to see Mr. and Mrs. Henderson pull into the yard. Mr. Henderson drove right up by the house, got out, walked up on the porch and turned on the yard light.

Mrs. Henderson got out of the car holding her nose. "What on earth is that awful smell?"

Mr. Henderson held the door to the house open for his wife. "Hurry up inside," he called. "I imagine something stirred up that old Skunk that lives under the pig shed."

Scooter, Shelly, and I giggled to ourselves as we pushed our bikes quietly down the driveway and out onto Mill Pond Road.

UNKOWN HEROES

✤ ✤ ✤

The next morning Shelly, Scooter, and I walked to school together. Along the way we agreed to keep silent about our part in the Zorro's revenge as we didn't want to get into a total war with the Skulls, but even then, the word had gotten out somehow and everyone was buzzing when we arrived at school the next morning. We had a ball listening to the various stories of what had happened and it was unbelievable how distorted a story can get.

"Hey you guys!" Art Hill called as we walked up the school steps. "Did you hear what happened last night?"

"What?" I said, faking interest.

Art's eyes grew wide when he discovered that he had an audience that hadn't heard the story yet. "Wow! You'll never believe this!"

"What happened!" we all shouted in unison.

"Old man Henderson...you know, Hacksaw? He caught Arnold, Bird legs, and Grease ball stealing apples and threw them right through the wall of his chicken coop!"

"No kidding!" I cried. "Did anyone get hurt?"

"Well, I heard Arnold might have a broken leg and the other two are all beaten up."

Barry Thomas walked up while Art was telling the story and listened patiently. When Art finished, Barry had to tell his version of what had happened.

"That isn't what I heard," he began. "I heard that the cops have been laying for those guys for a long time because they've been vandalizing the property of some of the old people in town. Arnold and those guys were out at the Henderson place and were going to push over the chicken coop when it caved in on them. Old man Henderson called the cops when he heard the noise and then held those guys at gunpoint until the cops got there."

"Where are you guys hearing all of these stories?" I asked.

"Sally Johnson, down at the cafe, saw the cops bring them in last night and she's been telling everyone in town about it."

By this time a small crowd of boys had gathered around and several had heard different stories, none of which were the truth.

Mike Bardill claimed he knew the real story because Sally Johnson was his aunt and she had called his mom last night when she saw the cops bring them in. "My Aunt Sally saw it all last night and she even overheard some of what the cops were saying. They were bringing them into the police station and said they were going to call their parents… And you guys want to know what was really weird?"

"What?" said everyone.

Mike looked around as if to make sure nobody else was listening. He then lowered his voice and said in a half-whisper, "They didn't have any clothes on!"

Everyone broke into howls of laughter! Two boys hit the ground holding their sides while the rest of us laughed until tears rolled down our cheeks.

That took the cake! Nothing could be possibly worse to a boy of our age than to be caught out in public without any clothes on. That was total humiliation!

At last the laughter died down and someone had the sense to ask the question as to why they didn't have any clothes on.

"Well," said Mike. "I heard that old man Henderson caught them stealing chickens from his chicken coop and forced them at gunpoint to take off their clothes and roll around in pig manure. While he was doing this, Mrs. Henderson called the cops and they came and picked them up."

This story brought another roar of laughter and tears were still rolling down our cheeks as we went up the steps with the opening bell.

None of the Skulls made it to school that day, lending more rumors to the events of the previous night. By the end of the day it was being told that Arnold and his buddies were being sent away to a juvenile prison and would be gone for the rest of the year. Scooter, Shelly, and I knew that these were all just stories and that they would probably be back in school the next day. We were sure that they most likely had to spend the day in a bathtub to get rid of Stinky's perfume.

That afternoon we walked slowly home from school, recalling to each other what each of us had felt the night before. It was interesting to listen to each other and note the different reactions we all had experienced to the same adventure. Shelly pretty much summed it up when she proclaimed. "Well, Arnold was right about one thing for sure in his speech to the class."

"What do you mean by that, Shell?" I asked.

"Remember…? Arnold said everyone would be hearing about and talking about the Skulls."

Scooter and I had a good laugh about that one. "Wow! Isn't that the truth?" Scooter exclaimed.

As we walked along in silence for a moment I suddenly realized an awareness that I was becoming more than a little fond of Shelly. I was seeing her in a whole new light and it was giving me a funny feeling. I smiled to myself as I was thinking and wondering if she felt anything like this.

Scooter was walking in the gutter kicking a big pile of leaves along in front of him. We were so caught up in our stories and the swishing leaves that we didn't hear the police car pull up right behind us. A short beep of the horn caused all of us to jump about a foot.

We turned in surprise just as Inspector 4 stepped out of the passenger side of the squad car. He had on his tan suit and dark glasses, just as we had seen him the other day. Only this time he didn't seem so scary.

"Hello Zorro's. Got a minute?" He asked.

"Yes sir," we all answered, thinking that maybe we might be in some kind of trouble yet.

Inspector 4 walked over to the sidewalk and removed his sun glasses. "I just want to thank you kids for helping solve this case and I want you to know that your names have been cleared."

Our shoulders slumped in relief. "Thank you sir," we said in unison.

Inspector 4 smiled and asked, "Did you kids set up that whole thing last night?"

"Yes sir," I said, "Scooter came up with most of the plan, but we all took part in setting it up."

"Well, I'd say it was carried out to perfection. I don't think those boys will be pulling any fast ones for a very long time."

"Are they going to prison?" Shelly asked.

Inspector 4 laughed. "No, I just mean I think they've learned a very good lesson and will be behaving themselves in the future. I warned them that the next time they won't be getting off so easy."

"I hope you don't think we're mean or something," I said. "We just wanted to teach Arnold a lesson for trying to get us into trouble with Mrs. Bronson."

"I know...I know, but I think you kids had better find a different way to do good deeds. With your luck I'd join the Boy Scouts or something."

"Yes sir. I think the Zorro's are done here in Ghost Lake and besides, I don't think we could top last night's case."

Inspector 4 laughed again. "No, I don't think so. You kids would make good policemen someday and we want to give you a little something for helping us."

Inspector 4 reached in the inside pocket of his tan suit and took out an envelope. He opened it and removed three slips of paper.

"Here are three gift certificates for five dollars each to the cafe in town. Buy yourselves some hamburgers, fries, and malts and keep the change."

Scooter, Shelly, and I looked at each other with wide eyes and raised eyebrows. "Wow! Thank you sir!"

"It's my pleasure," he said shaking our hands. "You kids have a good school year and thank you again."

"You're welcome sir."

Inspector 4 walked over to the squad car and turned to us once again. "Oh...by the way...Mr. Henderson asked me to tell you that he would like to see you again as soon as possible."

"I wonder what he wants." Scooter said as we watched the police car drive away.

"I hope he isn't mad at us for knocking down the shed," Shelly said.

"No," I assured her. "He told us he wanted to tear it down and he wanted us to help him. Whatever it is, I suppose we should go out there as soon as possible. I don't want to spend the rest of the week worrying about it."

"Me neither," Scooter agreed. "Why don't we go out there this evening?"

After talking it over, it was decided that tonight was as good as any. We agreed to meet at my house at five o'clock and ride out from there.

"Let's tell our moms that we're going to help Mr. Henderson finish picking his apples and that we might be a little late," I suggested.

"Good idea!" Scooter exclaimed. "See you at five."

By five-fifteen we were cresting Taylor's hill and cruising down toward the Henderson farm. It looked a lot quieter than the last time we had been here.

Mr. Henderson came out on the back porch as we pedaled up the driveway. Waving his arm he motioned us over to the house.

"Hello boys, and who do we have here?" He said pointing at Shelly.

"This is Shelly Patten, Mr. Henderson. She's a good friend of ours and came along for the ride."

"Well, I'm glad to meet you Shelly. We've just finished supper and you're just in time for some hot apple pie."

Naturally it would have been impolite to refuse his offer as we didn't want to hurt his feelings. A feeling of relief came over me as I realized that Mr. Henderson must not be mad at us or he wouldn't be offering us apple pie.

Mrs. Henderson turned out to be as nice as her husband and served us up huge slices of hot apple pie with a mound of vanilla ice cream on top. We didn't say two words as we attacked the pie.

In a while my pie was finished and I couldn't contain my curiosity any longer. "Oh by the way, Mr. Henderson. A police officer said you wanted to talk to us about something."

Mr. Henderson looked at us with a slight smile and a twinkle in his eye. "Yes...this morning when I went outside I found the shed roof caved in. I thought for a minute that it had caved in by itself, but then I found some very curious things. It was a real mystery."

"What did you find sir?" Scooter asked.

"Well, I found my stepladder in the middle of the wreckage, and as I was pulling it out I noticed that the live trap was inside the shed. I distinctly remember putting it alongside the outside wall. You boys remember that don't you?"

"Yes sir," we agreed.

"And then I saw a rope tied to the center post that had fallen. The rope ran through the wall and over to the dog house. It looked to me like someone had hidden in the dog house and pulled that center post out."

"Why would they want to do that?" I asked.

"That's what I couldn't figure out. So, I called the police to report that something fishy was going on and they came out and told me that they had been here last night. They also told me that you boys had been out here and that you would be better able to explain to me what had happened."

My mom had always told me that honesty was the best policy and I figured that now was as good a time as any to put it into effect.

"Well Mr. Henderson," I began, "It's a long story and perhaps we should start from the beginning."

As the sun dropped down over Taylor's hill we sat around Mr. Henderson's kitchen table and related our story from the beginning. Scooter and Shelly jumped in from time to time and told of their sides and Mr. and Mrs. Henderson got quite a kick out of hearing our tale.

"And that's the end of the story," I said leaning back in my chair.

"Well, it sounds to me like justice was served once again," Mr. Henderson said. "The real Zorro would have been proud of you kids...and if you still want to come out next Saturday, we can finish cleaning up what's left of the shed."

"Yes sir, Mr. Henderson. We'll be here! For now though, I think we had better get going before our mom's start getting worried."

As we walked out the back door to our bikes, we could still detect a faint odor of skunk in the back yard. Looking over toward the woods, I wondered where Old Stinky was at this moment. We turned and waved to Mr. Henderson standing on his back porch as we rode out of the driveway.

It was over. We stopped in the darkness at the top of Taylor's hill and looked back at the full moon rising over the Henderson farm. None of us spoke, not wanting to spoil the moment. There was a sense of another chapter of our childhood coming to a close. It went unsaid, but we realized that at this time next year we would be in junior high and would be expected to act in a different manner. At that moment I came to the conclusion that I didn't want to grow up. I wanted to spend the rest of my life chasing around with Scooter and Shelly, pretending something or other and solving imaginary mysteries. I gazed for a moment longer and then turned my bike and rode down the other side of Taylor's hill.

AUTHORS NOTE

✿ ✿ ✿

This book, "The Zorro Club", is the second book in the Ghost Lake Chronicles series, the first being "The Legend." All characters are fictional, based on childhood memories of mine, for I too was twelve years old in 1952. I have tried to bring a sense of what that time and era was like. If you enjoyed the book or would like to send a comment to me, I would very much like to hear from you. Send comments to: Ghostlakechron@hotmail.com